OF WOLF AND PEACE

OF WOLF AND PEACE

PROVIDENCE PARANORMAL COLLEGE BOOK THREE

D.R. PERRY

This book is a work of fiction. All of the characters, organizations, and events portrayed in this novel are either products of the author's imagination or are used fictitiously. Sometimes both.

LMBPN Publishing
PMB 196, 2540 South Maryland Pkwy
Las Vegas, NV 89109

Version 2.0 May, 2021
ebook ISBN: 978-1-64971-699-6
Print ISBN: 978-1-64971-700-9

CHAPTER ONE

Josh

"Get up, Josh." The voice was loud, intense, and familiar. But I couldn't place it, not even after opening my eyes. The room was pitch black.

"Fine." I sat up as fast as I could, swinging and hoping my fist would make contact with whoever wanted to drag me out of bed at zero dark thirty in the morning. No luck.

"Out the window." Some invisible force pushed the middle of my back, propelling me out of bed. Magic? At least I wore pajamas a week into February. I still couldn't place the voice. Male, for sure.

"Light." If I saw who it was, maybe I could put up a fight.

"No. Get out of here right now." The voice had lowered to a near whisper, but all the intensity was still there. Someone I knew from school?

"Clothes." The hair on the back of my neck stood up. The rest of the house should have been dead silent at this hour. Instead, a whole slew of people stomped around the living room, the kitchen, the parlor. It was worse than the night our parents went to Block Island and Derek threw a party. This didn't sound like a bunch of 18-year-olds trying to get their illegal drink on, though.

"No time." The voice was on the other side of the room now, in the shadows near the closet.

"I'll go if you fess up to this later, man." I reached under the bed and grabbed the strap of my bug-out bag. After that, I stepped into my boots, not bothering to lace them.

"Fine. The window." I heard soft footfalls in the corner, then tumblers in a lock and a door opening. But my closet didn't have a lock. Heavy footsteps on the stairs killed the urge to investigate.

My room had a wannabe balcony, but I didn't use that. I'd need more than just stucco to get three stories down. I went to the smaller window, jerking on the shade to get it to snap up. It fell on my head instead. I pressed my lips closed, not daring to shout the string of epithets that had only gotten more colorful since I'd started at PPC.

Once I'd flipped the latch on the window, I wriggled out. The trellis had held my weight the last time I'd tried this, but I'd been fifteen and at least twenty pounds lighter back then. The top held up, but once I got to the second floor, it gave out. I thought of Tony Gitano the cat shifter as I fell to the ground, not remotely on my feet but relatively unharmed. I'd landed in the roses, all bare branches and thorns—the opposite of a comfortable landing. The cuts and scratches on my arms and face would heal in a few minutes. It was good to be a shifter.

I looked up. No one was at the window. The light went on upstairs in my room, along with shouts of surprise and barked orders to find me. I took off across the back lawn as fast as I could on two legs, and that was pretty damn fast. I'd won all the shifter-designated sprints they had in Track and Field back in High School.

The wall at the back of our property was too tall to hop

without shifting. The last thing I wanted to do was turn into a wolf in the middle of Providence. It'd make me easier to track, I'd lose all my stuff, and I'd have no idea when I'd be able to come back here. I hoped my parents were just doing a drill or something, but this could also be mutiny. They'd made a few unpopular decisions, and I hadn't helped their image lately. I turned right to beat feet toward the old garden gate. It was covered with ivy and I'd have to crawl through, but I should make it. I'd gained only twenty pounds since I was fifteen, not fifty.

The tiny gate still didn't have a lock, but the latch was on the inside of the wall. No one outside could reach it. My sister Beth always called it the Alice gate because it reminded her of something out of one of Lewis Carrol's books. I looked back at the house. Her room was lit up like a Christmas Tree. They'd gotten her, then. No way she could have put on her prosthetic in time to bug out unless whoever had warned me went to her first. Derek's windows were dark. He'd been missing since 2008.

I wriggled through the Alice gate, dragging the bag behind me. Once through, it clanged shut like a mouth full of metal teeth. No going back now. I looked at the sky, to find not even a trace of dawn. Time to visit Henry Baxter, then. He was my Beta though an unconventional one. Henry was a vampire, and wolf shifters'd had nothing to do with them since the early 1990s. I'd thought it was time to change that. My parents couldn't outright say they agreed even though I knew they did. I went down the street as fast as I could without attracting attention, doubling back so I didn't walk past the house.

My family estate was on the Upper East Side of Providence, a swanky neighborhood. Henry lived in a basement apartment most of the way down College Hill on the Lower East Side. It had just been renovated after a freaky Seelie hunting hound called a Spite tore a hole in the wall trying to get at him. We'd had trouble with a mind-controlled Summoner over Winter Break. Yeah, Extrahuman society was a bitch, but we dealt with it, my family especially. Mom and Dad did police work, and I'd be expected to follow in their footsteps.

I walked down Rochambeau Street, the most direct and often used way to get down to the Lower East Side. The more well-traveled my route, the better. It'd be easier to hide my trail. As I turned down the cross-street that would take me to Henry's place, a stream of intricately gorgeous music flowed from the first-floor window of a familiar triple-decker house. I turned around to see the light on, warmly incandescent and inviting. Usually, I didn't like violins, too squeaky, but whoever was playing managed to eliminate that particular sound from the mix.

I stepped forward, feeling a strong need to go and listen more closely. I didn't stop to think about why anyone in their right mind would give a masterwork solo violin performance on Rochambeau Street at who knows when in the morning. It smacked of compulsion, something you do in a dream or see in a horror movie, the kind where you yell at the screen about how dumb the guy walking toward the monster is, then roll your eyes and sit back to wait for him to die gruesomely. Yup, I was doing the future dead guy shuffle.

"Josh? What are you doing out at this hour?" I hadn't known my eyes were sore until I saw Nox Phillips. The sight of her snapped me right out of whatever weird trance the music had put me in. "Are those pajamas?" She blinked, almost as though she'd been enthralled by the music, too. I thought of something else that got people killed in horror movies.

"Um, yeah." I took a deep breath, trying to keep from blushing. The Kelpie was just about the most gorgeous girl I'd ever laid eyes on, tall and lean with dark hair and deep blue eyes. Unfortunately, dating any type of Changeling or Faerie was absolutely forbidden, even the shifters. Packs couldn't take sides in the conflict between the Unseelie Goblin King and the Seelie Sidhe Queen.

The pit of my stomach sank as I realized Nox had majorly

crossed the Queen and I'd been standing right there while she'd done it. Maybe the home invasion had more to do with me than I'd originally thought. At least I could ignore the fiddler now. "Had to bug out. Something nuts is going down at my house. Was on the way to find Henry."

"He's out of town until tomorrow, remember? Went to Vermont with Maddie for the weekend." Nox shook her head a little more vigorously than most people do when indicating the negative. Was she shaking off the music's effects, too?

"Crap on a crap cracker." I ran my hand over the top of my head, hoping it'd stand up in a less bed-head kind of way. "I got nowhere to go, and I need to figure out what happened, why people are chasing me."

"Why not come back to campus, then?" She put one hand on my shoulder. "Wait for the rest of Tinfoil Hat to wake up and talk to them about it. Whoever's looking for you wouldn't think to check the Nocturnal Lounge."

"Good idea." Tinfoil Hat was the temporary pack I'd made during the Summoner situation. It was a motley crew but still had mostly shifters as members. "Lead on."

I walked, trying not to brush against Nox when the sidewalk narrowed halfway to campus. It wouldn't be right to give her the wrong idea. Then again, I wasn't even sure whether she thought of me that way. Kelpies were Unseelie magical horse shifters, freshwater versions of the Seelie seal shifter Selkies. They could be inscrutable, especially while wearing the magical pelt that gives them their powers. Some of them had magic or psychic powers as well. I had no idea whether Nox did or not.

"Hey, Nox. I just remembered you never said whether you had any magic or whatever before the Kelpie thing."

"No, I didn't." She pulled out her phone, tapping out a text message.

"So? Dish." I put my hands on my hips before realizing how

ridiculous that looked while walking uphill in pajamas and combat boots.

She just laughed. We turned up Angell Street, heading toward Thayer Street and the old trolley tunnel. The entrance to the Nocturnal Lounge was in there, with a secret knock to open the hidden door. They ran the place like they thought it was the Bat Cave or something. Maybe there were actual bats or bat shifters or even Batman, and I just didn't know. I'd only been in there once, right after a Grim had wrecked it in more of that Summoner business. When the door opened, and we went up the stairs, I knew this time would be different from the last. I heard music and smelled pizza. My stomach growled almost as viciously as I could while shifted.

Henry's usual study and work spot in the mezzanine was empty, of course. Sometimes, Tony was up there, but not now. The vampire band Night Creatures practiced on the bottom floor, blasting out riffs behind Lane belting out *Of Wolf and Man* by Metallica. A mixed crowd of Unseelie Changelings, vampires, and nocturnal shifters stood or sat, listening. I finally saw a familiar face and headed down the stairs. Nox followed. She'd have to keep an eye on me because only the night people could be in here without an escort.

I headed straight for the counter at the side of the room, grabbing the last slice of pizza before Fred Redford could. The Redcap Changeling frowned at my hand, then grinned when he saw who it belonged to. He didn't bother trying to talk over the band, just picked up the Leaning Tower of Pizza he'd already taken off the tray to get out of the way of the Skeleton Crew. Ghostly hands that only Psychic Mediums and Death Magi could see removed the empty box. They'd replace it with another one in the not too distant future. Ghost employees unlived all over the PPC campus. According to the Psychic Mediums that was a good thing. It kept them busy until they could move on and was one of the reasons fewer hauntings happened on College Hill than most other areas of a city as old as Providence.

Nox grabbed cups and a bottle of root beer, following Fred and me back to the mezzanine. I'd known Fred since preschool. Even though we never went to each other's house after school or anything, we ran in lots of the same circles. I wasn't allowed to call him a friend but knew we would have been if my parents didn't run the two most important packs in the city. Mom headed the Extrahuman Task Force for the city police and Dad ran PPC Campus Police. The only way they'd need to be more impartial was if they worked for the DA.

We sat at Henry's table. It was quieter there when the Night Creatures practiced. We could actually hear each other talk in that corner. I let Fred eat half of his pizza first, then explained how I'd been dragged out of bed and ended up here. He chewed thoughtfully for a few moments. I sat waiting for his reaction, sipping root beer and wishing it had a shot of Jägermeister in it. No one could bust me for drinking. The gap year I'd taken before starting at PPC meant I was twenty-one in my sophomore year.

"Sounds like a mutiny. Better lie low and stay out of it." Fred adjusted the red Paw Sox cap he always wore, then chomped down another slice of pizza with eerily perfect teeth. "Worst that can happen is your folks get busted down from Alpha and have to run as part of the regular pack for a while, right?"

"Not exactly." I sighed into my root beer. "Thing is, they could get kicked out altogether depending on whether whoever did this gives them a fair challenge."

"That's nuts. It's not like they killed someone, right?" Fred brushed his hands over the now empty plate. I wondered where he'd put it all. He was about the same size as most bear shifters, but without the metabolism drain of shifting, I couldn't imagine how he used all those calories.

"No. No killing since before they took over, during an assignment at the Boston Internment." I put my hands flat on the table in front of me.

"It sounds more like a raid than a mutiny" I heard a plastic crack from Nox's direction, punctuating her statement. She held a brown paper bag over my cup and tilted it. "Shh. Don't tell or everyone will want some."

As she repeated the process over Fred's cup and then her own, I smelled rum. It wasn't Jaeger, but it'd do. I tried not to smile too much, just topped us all off with more root beer. I sipped, my shoulders instantly relaxing. My mind cleared too, letting me think more about what she'd said. A raid? There sure had been enough people in the house for that.

"Maybe you're right, Nox. It was like a raid, like the ATF or the FBI came in. Except it wasn't those agencies. I didn't smell flash-bangs or guns." I took another sip of the oddly satisfying drink.

"Anyone in your parents' pack have connections to those?" Fred gulped down half his spiked root beer.

"No. Not that I know of." I shrugged. "Everyone's police of some kind, but no Federal anything. This is Rhode Island, after all."

"Yeah, local focus." Nox chewed on her lower lip. "Not so easy to deal with some iffier elements if they think RICO's watching."

"Huh. You sound like my dad." Fred grimaced around another mouthful of pizza. He swallowed that before continuing. "And everyone knows he used to be connected a million ways from Sunday."

"Yeah. Gives my folks a nice headache because there's nothing to balance that out on the other side of things if you catch my drift." I knew better than to say the word Seelie out loud in the Nocturnal Lounge.

"Hey, we can't help it if we're better at that kind of thing than they are, in this neck of the woods." Fred held his hands out palms up, then frowned down at his empty plate. "They're too hidebound for anything but high society, and around here Hertha Harcourt has that element locked down."

"Dragon shifters don't let go of anything once they've got their hooks in. Tenacious." Nox seemed to look everywhere but at me. Neither of us was about to tell Fred how the dragon lady's son and heir was in my pack. "The whole Faerie population's unbalanced lately. Unseelies deal with change way better than they do."

I had to keep quiet while I swallowed my anger. Blaine Harcourt was one of the smartest people I knew, but still vying for Omega in Tinfoil Hat. He'd figured out that some disruptive element was messing with PPC and maybe all the Extrahumans in Providence months ago. He'd also decided to try to make Nox his latest conquest. She was a big girl and could make her own decisions, but nothing said I had to be happy about it. Blaine was a playboy and would stay that way until his mother told him who to marry. Some guys might have been okay with that, knowing he'd move along once he was done with her. I wasn't. Nox deserved better than to be treated like a toy. But I had no right to complain. It wasn't like I could offer her anything myself. Forbidden relationships were forbidden.

Fred glanced back and forth between us like he watched a tennis match, or maybe Forrest Gump playing ping pong. Probably the ping pong. I sighed, then kicked back all my rum and root beer. Nox didn't look at me, but she gave me a refill. I drank that, too, straight. I saw her take a shot directly from the bottle out of the corner of my eye.

"Whatever that was, I'm staying out of it." Fred picked up his plate. "Pizza calls. Maybe those ghosts will surprise me with a stack of bacon cheeseburgers instead some night."

The silence Fred left behind was the opposite of comfortable. I sat in it with Nox for a little while because nothing I could break it with was what I really wanted to say.

CHAPTER TWO

Nox

I was about to pass the rest of the rum to Josh and leave when Tony showed up with Blaine in tow. The dragon shifter smiled at us, then dropped me a wink. I'd have to sit there and let Josh's hackles rise and fall without comment. We needed Blaine's brain on this, so Josh would just have to deal with his jealousy issues. I wasn't interested in the dragon shifter, but any time I tried to talk to Josh about it, he shut me down. It was one of the most confusing things I'd ever seen, and being a Kelpie meant my ancestors' attitudes were constantly humming in the background.

"You called, we answered." Blaine sat down across from me, leaning his elbows on the table. "What did you need me for, Nox?"

"We'll need the rest of Tinfoil Hat when they wake up, too. Josh has a problem." I put the bottle to my lips, killing the rum myself. Liquid courage. I might be a Kelpie, but a magical Unseelie horse was small potatoes next to a dragon.

"You mean a problem besides thinking pajamas go with combat boots instead of a smoking jacket?" Blaine waggled his eyebrows.

"Knock it off." Tony sat down next to Blaine, rolling his eyes. "He had to bug out in the middle of the night. I bet you'd look even sillier." Tony put his head in his hands. "I can't believe I'm sticking up for a wolf shifter in public like this."

I laughed instead of sharing with the group that I'd never texted Tony. Well, it was sort of me covering for the cat shifter. I only half wanted to. The other half of that reaction came from Grandpa. He was the most recent and strongest influence on my magic pelt. Being a Kelpie was kind of a bum deal because someone parental was always watching unless you put the pelt away for a while. It took endless amounts of compromise and battle picking. Laughing at a joke was one I'd gladly lose if it meant I could fight him on something more important later. It was also hell on any attempt at feminine grooming. Styling my hair or makeup was as futile as resisting the Borg. A constant frizz-inducing dampness clung to my scalp, and even waterproof mascara ran like the wind under the pelt's influence.

"Oh. You texted Tony, too?" I wondered why Josh sounded so relieved about that. Why would it make any difference whether I got in touch with Tony or Blaine? I let cat-boy answer.

"Yeah. Guaranteed to be awake all night, you know." Tony Gitano was lucky none of us were Telepathic Psychics. I only knew he was lying because I'd forgotten to message him.

"Yeah. Unless you're bird watching." Someone would have to be the butt of Blaine's jokes tonight. After Intersession, the whole pack knew Tony had a soft spot for a certain owl shifter.

"What's that supposed to mean?" Tony blinked, his pupils narrowing into something resembling catlike slits.

"Nothing at all. Just groggy. Too bad you couldn't just let

sleeping dragons lie." Blaine pulled an iPad out of his backpack. "Ah, the curse of being the brainiac."

"Thought that was Frampton's nickname, Trogdor." Josh gave a Lynn-worthy snort.

"True enough." He powered up the tablet, propping it up in its case so he could use the attached keyboard. "Can't we lose the old Strongbad moniker, though? Call me Smaug or something a little more classic?"

"How about Puff? You are magic and live by the sea, after all." I smiled mildly.

"Trogdor's fine." Blaine cracked his knuckles and started typing. "Okay, Josh. What happened?"

I listened to Josh's story again, trying to think of anything that hadn't occurred to me before. A mutiny still seemed most likely, but why? Could it be the alliance he'd made with Henry? No. The response to that had been overwhelmingly supportive. Since Henry had been a Psychic, wasn't an old vampire, and had no Faerie heritage, he was an excellent choice for the first new alliance since the Big Reveal. Coincidence had been on our side this winter. I gently knocked on the wooden bottom of the table, hoping that trend would continue as we moved into spring.

"Tell me again about wolf shifter politics and moon phases." Blaine scratched his chin. "I know there's something about moon phases and leadership, but can't remember what, exactly."

"See, this is why Lynn's the brainiac and you're Trogdor the dragon man. She'd remember that." Josh leaned back in his chair, glancing down at my now empty rum bottle. "It's the new moon tonight. I've been so out of it I didn't even think. That changes things by a mile."

"How so?" I tossed my dearly departed rum bottle into the wastepaper basket in the corner by the bookcases. "Three points. Anyway, continue."

"New moons are the one time packmates can apprehend an Alpha, but then it makes no sense for them to take my sister and stomp into my room. My parents are the real Alphas. No offense, guys, but Tinfoil Hat's not considered the real thing in wolf shifter terms."

"What could it be, though?" Tony scratched his head, then tucked a strand of hair behind one ear. He seemed stumped, but my ancestors noticed something flat in his voice. I wondered whether he shared my suspicion. Now I understood why Grandpa wanted to cover for him. Maybe he'd cover for me now. "Couldn't be about that whole Summoner problem over winter break, could it?"

"Well, your parents did arrest that Summoner for murder. What did they find at his house? Anything that might be a problem for the pack or police?" Blaine tapped his fingers on the table. "He had Anchors for pure Faeries, both, um…not the variety that comes in here."

"Huh." Josh leaned forward, palms on the table. "I'm not sure what they found. There'll be a list down at Campus Police, though."

"Good. Then someone can check in the morning." Blaine blew a smoke ring.

"Don't you mean I can check in the morning?" Josh clenched his jaw.

"That might be a bad idea." Blaine raised an eyebrow. "Unless you want to end up wherever they've got the rest of your family. The moon's technically still new for a couple more days. Anyway, since you're not a real Alpha. You have to lie low. They could snatch you anytime. Might want to avoid the general campus until you know it's safe."

"That's one week. I can't do anything to defend my family's honor until the half-moon." Josh put his head in his hands. "I'm going to flunk a mid-term."

"Why?" Blaine typed something on his iPad. "Haven't you been studying?"

"No." Josh sighed. "I slacked off, and our brainiac, Lynn, can't help me. This exam is shifter-specific and physical."

"I'll do whatever I can." I wanted to put my arm around him. I fought with Grandpa until he let me punch Josh's shoulder instead. My ancestors always fought me on displays of affection toward men. "School of hard Nox is in session."

"I'll help, too." Tony grinned, his eyes going back to normal. "School of homework fetching over here, for the other classes. Also, a little more neutral than Kelpie school, just in case."

"Oh, good point." Blaine tapped the table again. His toothy grin reminded me more of a crocodile than an oligarch. Grandpa thought those were almost the same thing.

"Maybe." I peered across the table at Blaine. "What time is it, anyway? I have an early class on Tuesdays."

"Almost five." Blaine shut down his iPad. "I should get out of here, head back to the dorm. I have a plan about how to get the information from Campus Police involving Olivia, but I need to find her before breakfast. Extrahuman Law students can access their files. Where are you staying, Josh?"

"With me." Fred loomed behind Tony. "Dad's at a job on Block Island. Only people home all week are me, Mom, and my kid brother. They're Psychics and I'm untithed, so all good on the Faerie neutrality front just in case."

"How did you know all that? You were down there in that noise stuffing your face." Tony glanced up, doing his cat shifter bristle.

"Ears." Fred stuck his hand under the table and pulled something off. "See?" He held up a small gray triangle, then stuck it on the side of his head. I watched the shimmer of falling Glamour as it dropped, revealing his true appearance.

Everyone else besides me gasped. Tony's reaction was slightly delayed. Redcaps had gray skin, red eyes, slightly pointed ears, and a set of perfectly even teeth so white they were almost blue. Fred almost looked like one, a sign he'd used faerie magic so much he'd need to tithe to a Monarch soon. Once he'd put the top of his ear back on, Fred's Glamour came back, rounding his ears and changing his skin back to its usual Mediterranean olive tone. I tried not to look at Tony, wondering why he'd covered for himself like that. With the amount of time he spent in the Nocturnal Lounge and his Nocturnal History major, he'd have studied Changelings by now, surely?

"Wow. How much longer are you going to be able to put off tithing and taking your Mantle?" Grandpa's question slipped out before I could censor myself. He'd done that to me all through Magic Theory during Winter Intersession. At least Chuck, Ian, and Maddie had taken it in stride. It wasn't something I liked doing in front of Josh, though.

"Maybe summer." Fred didn't even grin. "I was hoping to get through the Fall semester before I have to spend a year and a day in the Under. Now I'll be lucky to make it through Spring."

"We'll miss you." Tony's voice cracked a little. "Whenever it's time, I mean." I wondered what the cat man wasn't saying.

"That's mutual, squirt." Fred flicked Tony on the side of the head. "Anyway, we'd better get going before the sun comes up, Josh. You probably don't want to be on the street in your PJs in broad daylight."

"Yeah." Josh got up, shouldering his bag. He looked me right in the eye. "I'll call you later." He ignored the light haze of smoke coming from Blaine's direction. "Got to let you know what I need help with."

I nodded, not breaking eye contact with him even though Grandpa wanted me to. He didn't much like how interested I was in Josh. I didn't care. I waited to break eye contact until he had to turn and follow Fred. Blaine packed up and left, too. Tony sat diagonally from me across the table. I kept my eyes on Josh until he was out of sight, making the cat wait.

"Why are you still here, Tony?" I finally looked at him, startled at the anger flashing in his bright green and vertically slitted eyes. I'd gotten his inner cat up, but had no idea why.

"Because you need to know Josh's biggest problem, and I didn't want to deal with him freaking out over it." I studied him. His face, posture, and voice all seemed genuine enough. I gave in to Grandpa, this time, and let him nudge me into using a little Kelpie charm. Tony's pupils dilated slightly, still cat-vertical but more relaxed.

"All right. I'm listening." I folded my hands on the tabletop.

"Faerie neutrality." Tony took a deep breath. "It's his part in releasing that Sprite over Intersession that's screwing things up for his family."

"But that's on me. Josh didn't do anything but stand there." I'd been the one to undo the enchantment on the poor creature. I'd even stolen the means to do it right out of Blaine's backpack. Grandpa made me shudder. Risky business, stealing from a dragon shifter, even a young one.

"He stood by and let you do it. As your Alpha, he's responsible." Tony made a noise halfway between a sigh and a hiss. "And whose idea was it, anyway?"

"Mine." I would have fidgeted, but Grandpa kept me still.

"Bull." Tony's eyes narrowed.

"All right, you got me." I shrugged the shoulder Grandpa had relinquished to my control. "Josh actually had the idea that freeing the Sprite would stop it. So what?" He'd thought of it right after I saw that funny little Gnome, but Tony didn't have to know that.

"Josh took a side. He's heir to two of the biggest shifter authorities in the city. He's supposed to be neutral, but he sided with you, an Unseelie shifter. And then, he let you take a Gnome's advice." He stared, unblinking.

"He did it to save his Beta. Nothing more." I gripped the edge of the table, wondering how he knew about the Gnome with the metal teeth. "We stopped a murderer. No one should complain about that."

"If that's true, why didn't he turn the Sprite in?"

"That Sprite owes us all. He'd have lost favors from a Pure Faerie." That should have been perfectly reasonable as far as the Faerie Courts were concerned.

"You tell me how that looks." Tony put his hands flat on the table.

"Bad." I closed my eyes. "Like he's the Alpha they were actually after, not his parents." I held my breath for a moment. "But he said they don't consider him a real Alpha, right?"

"Not right. That idea lives in Understatement City." Tony dragged his nails against the tabletop, leaving faint grooves. "Him trusting your judgment has to be the reason for all this. Josh's problem is you. Dump him."

"Huh?" I blinked and swallowed at the same time.

"Break up with him, Yoko." Tony's glare was almost palpable.

"But we're not even going out. I don't even think he likes me that way." I knew I was wrong the second the words came out of my mouth. Why else would he be jealous of Blaine?

"Bull." I heard a muffled squeak as Tony ground his teeth. "Leave the pack then."

"What's the big deal about it for you anyway, Tony Gitano?" I leaned back in my chair, unable to stop Grandpa from saying what he wanted. "You're the shadiest, dodgiest person I've ever seen. There's an awful lot of rule-bending in your family. Plus, you knew about the Gnome. I never breathed a word of that to anyone. What if you're the problem?"

Tony's eyes got big, and his face paled. Something between a hiss and a growl rumbled at the back of his throat. He opened his mouth, then closed it again without saying anything. His nails made a splintery sound against the table. He lifted them up, holding his hands palms out in a gesture of concession, possibly even surrender. He stood, backing away from me. The mantle on his duster drooped as though he'd been out in the rain. I didn't understand why right away until I felt water dripping from my hair to my shoulders.

"Jeez Tony, I'm sorry." I struggled to get my hand to my stomach, fighting Grandpa every step of the way to release myself from the grasp of my pelt. I pulled it off, rolled it up, put it away in the oilcloth in my rucksack. "Look, it's just me now. No more ancestors."

"Are you sure that was all them?" He shivered a little. I didn't blame him. Grandpa's spell would freak out any feline. Kelpie Water magic was one reason I'd enrolled at PPC. I needed to learn how to control it. Cat shifters were scared of water, and all my ancestors knew it. Still, Tony seemed even worse off than expected, like he'd come close to drowning before.

"Almost all. Look, it's obvious you're hiding something most of the time, but I don't think you're the problem. And that was an unfair low blow, mentioning your family like that. I'm sorry, Tony."

"Yeah. And I'm sorry, too." He sat back down, but only on the edge of the seat. "Look, if we're going to get Josh out of this and avoid a huge Extrahuman conflict, we need to be honest without attacking each other."

"You sound like a diplomat."

"I kind of am. Supposed to be if I can ever—" He blinked, eyes redder than they should be. Was he on the verge of tears? "But anyway." He cleared his throat. "I wouldn't be surprised if this has something to do with Blaine's Extramagus. Remember what Henry found in his amulet? An Extramagus around his age, with a possible connection to that Stanhope family. We need to look at that, find out what happened to them."

"If they're Magi, what would they have to do with wolf shifters?"

"Could be plenty. That kid Henry described was blond. So was Stanhope. So's Josh for that matter. Maybe there's a relation there. Magi used to marry into any Extrahuman family they could back in the day. Have you ever seen his parents? Pictures of his siblings?"

"He has siblings?" I blinked. He'd never mentioned them.

"Two. One's been missing for years. The other's missing a leg, the sister he mentioned. That's why he inherits the packs even though he's the youngest." Tony spoke without quite meeting my eyes, head tilted slightly to the side as though hearing something I couldn't.

"How do you know all this?"

"Coincidence, convergence, and conniving. One of the reasons all that stuff you said freaked me out so much is because it's a little true. I am dodgy and shady. I have too many secrets to keep that aren't mine. The ones that do belong to me…well. Voices carry. I can't risk mentioning them."

"The cat man who knew too much?" I quirked an eyebrow.

"Yeah. Curiosity kills." His lips stretched into a thin, flat line.

"Let's hope satisfaction works like an AED." I sighed. "So, what do we do now?"

"Go to class. Get information. Help Josh study. Wait for Trogdor and the brain to puzzle it out."

"All that in a week, huh?" I shook my head.

"Yeah. Let's hope it's a long one." Tony got up, stretching and clearly more at ease than he'd been just a few minutes before. "It'll be a long day, at least. Maybe I'll have time to catch a cat nap this afternoon."

"Same here, minus the cat part." I stifled a yawn. "Hopefully, Josh won't call in the middle of that."

He did, of course.

CHAPTER THREE

Josh

I thought I'd gotten the wrong number when a huge yawn answered. I checked the screen to find I hadn't.

"Whoozat?" Nox's slurred voice came in crystal clear. I tried to imagine her just after a nap, fluffing sleep-tousled hair and stretching limber arms over her head. What would she wear to sleep? I cleared my throat, ending that line of thought as fast as I could.

"Just Josh. Calling about homework." I held my tongue. Couldn't say much of anything else. "I can read you a list whenever you're ready."

"Go ahead." I heard the clack of a keyboard and a muffled conversation over the clink of silverware.

"Wait a minute, Nox." I felt my brow ridging like a Ruffles potato chip. "Were you sleeping in the dining hall?"

"No." I heard her hand cover the phone as she told someone

she didn't want any more coffee. "Why would I do a thing like that?"

"Dunno. Are you in a cafe or something? You know what, never mind." I sighed. I'd have to call Bobby or Lynn and ask them to check on her. Or maybe Maddie once she got back from Vermont. I'd even call Jeannie if I had to. I rattled off the list of classes, Professors, and office hours I'd prepared earlier.

"Okay. I'll talk to Tony. He can bring your homework for everything besides Shifter Mastery." I heard her take a sip of something. "For that, we should meet. I don't think Tony will give you much of a challenge sparring."

"But where?" I ran a hand over my head, spiking up my hair. "I'm not supposed to go to campus, remember?" There was a long pause like Nox was thinking or struggling with some idea.

"I'll think of something."

"Fine." I wondered why she didn't just ask Bobby for help with that and then remembered. He'd be taking the freshman version of Shifter Mastery. If he practiced with me, he'd get too worn out to handle his coursework. "I gotta go."

"Bye." She hung up.

I wished I could talk to Beth. I'd tried, but her phone went straight to voicemail, and there was no response to my texts. I shook my head, still unable to think of a reason they'd take her. Beth's losses meant she wasn't even in the running for Beta of either pack in the future. I missed her, even more than when she'd been down the hall. At least I knew she could hear my knocking on the door and requests to come out and do something. If any of them hurt my sister, they'd be outcasts the minute I took over. She'd been through enough. I got up and headed toward the door of the Redfords' attic guest room. I nearly bumped into Fred's younger brother in the doorway.

"Sorry, kid." I felt like a jerk because I'd forgotten his name.

"You need to say more of what you mean and mean more of what you say." The kid's eyes were round as saucers. I could barely see his irises, they were so dilated. Did the Redford family Psychic ability come with fortune cookie one-liners and involve mainlining eyedrops?

"Um, okay." I shrugged, still looking down at him. Had I ever been that tiny? "Anything else?"

"Oh! Sorry." The kid blinked and shook his head. His eyes went back to normal. "Mom says there're sandwiches downstairs if you're hungry." He stepped out of the doorway.

"Thanks, kid." I stepped into the hall and headed toward the stairs.

"My name's Ed." He smirked up at me, looking like he knew I couldn't remember his name.

"Awesome." So, the Redfords were the type of people who made their kids' names rhyme. Who'd have thought?

Downstairs was cozy but well-crafted like the rest of the house. Fred's dad didn't own the most successful Extrahuman contracting business for nothing. Redford Renovations did everything from building entire houses with magical accouterments to outfitting old homes with magical devices to accommodate disabilities. He'd sent a crew over to re-do half our estate after Beth lost her leg. That had been harrowing because she'd also lost her fiancé, Ren Ichiro. He'd been from a Tanuki family, though not a shifter. Tanuki and their kin were supposed to be the luckiest people on the planet. I wondered whether he'd given up all his Luck so she could live through the wreck on the Newport Bridge.

In the kitchen, the dining table, sideboard, island, and every counter was covered with plates of sandwiches. I spotted just about every combination of bread and filling you could think of. I almost told Mrs. Redford she didn't have to go to that kind of trouble for little old me when Fred walked in. He sat at the table, pulling six plates close to him and glancing up with a territorial spark in his eye.

"*Mangia*!" Mrs. Redford's accent was deep Cranston, with

long, nasal vowel sounds. Unexpected, considering her hair was much smaller than most ladies from that part of Rhode Island. "Sit. Eat. You're skinny, even for a wolf shifter. At least you've got more meat on you than that scrawny Gitano boy my Fred works with."

"Yes, ma'am." I picked up a ham and swiss on rye and sat across from Fred, noticing he'd already polished off five plates. He pulled the sixth toward him. I wasn't going to bother asking where he put it all. Redcaps ate even more than their untithed Changeling offspring. Mrs. Redford was probably used to making more than twice this much lunch.

"You call Nox yet?" Fred enunciated surprisingly well around the mouthful of sandwich.

"He did." Ed sat on a stool by the island, a bologna sandwich on Wonderbread clutched in one pint-sized hand.

"Well, that's good." Fred swallowed a mouthful of the meatball sub. "Except for the part where you listened in on a guest."

"Sorry, but Rob wanted me to." Ed glanced up toward the lazily spinning ceiling fan.

"Rob, schmob." Mrs. Redford was there, looming over Ed. "How many times have I told you to be careful of that one? Loves to get you into trouble."

"I know Mom, but he said it was important." Ed sighed, looking at something or someone near the ceiling. "Rob says Josh has a big problem. He needs to do everything right, or he's going to be in serious danger."

"Is this true, Rob?" Mrs. Redford looked right where Ed did. She waited, reminding me for all the world of someone using a Bluetooth earbud. Her eyes dilated just like Ed's had. After a moment, she sighed and turned to pat the kid on the head. "You're right this time, bambino. But next time, don't just go taking Rob's word for anything without asking me first, okay?"

"All right, Mama." Ed crammed the last of his sandwich in his mouth. "Can I go play now?"

"Sure." She glared at the spot I assumed Rob occupied instead of her younger son's retreating form. "You stay here with me. Let the boy be a boy, not a conduit." She glanced at me. "You, too." How had she known I'd been about to escape with a second sandwich?

"What's up, Mrs. Redford?" I took a bite of this new confection of bread and filling, waiting for her to talk. Velvet Elvis. My tongue stuck to the roof of my mouth.

"Rob's connected to the ghost of a Precognitive. He doesn't usually see things happening to the living, but he did this time. You want to know why?"

"Sure. Go ahead." That's right, the mom and the kid were Mediums. I hadn't paid much attention to Psychic wooj before making one of the vampiric variety my Beta.

"You or someone you care about will die if you don't correct your course." She picked what looked like prosciutto and provolone on ciabatta off the top of one of the plates. "Maybe both."

"I'll take that into account." My voice came out all mushy because the peanut butter still stuck to the roof of my mouth. What a canine predicament. I glanced around for a drink. I moved toward a glass and the water pitcher. "Thanks."

"Whatever Ed said to you upstairs was important." Mrs. Redford got between me and the water, her gaze intense over the top of her bread, cheese, and meat. "Do whatever he told you, and you might come through this in better shape than your sister did the last time Rob declared a dire prediction."

"Wait, what?" I almost dropped my sandwich. "What's Beth got to do with this?"

"She didn't listen, even though I warned her myself." Mrs. Redford shook her head. "Thought a bad foretelling would go away because the Ichiros are what they are. But you know how that turned out. Don't let it happen to you, too. Coincidence only makes it more likely that prediction will come true."

"Ugh." Fred reached for a BLT on multigrain. "Coincidence is a bitch, and then you die."

"Language, Frederick Raymond Redford, or you eat outside." Mrs. Redford reached one hand toward a rack of wooden spoons.

"Sorry, Mama." Fred put the sandwich down and folded his hands on the crumb-strewn table in front of him.

"First strike today. Just be good." She dropped her hand, then poured three glasses of water.

"I will, Mama." Fred picked his half-eaten sandwich up and ate it in one bite. Then, he gulped his water down in one go. "And thanks for lunch."

"Don't forget who else you should thank." Mrs. Redford glanced at the stack of plates floating toward the sink. They seemed to rinse and place themselves gently in the dishwasher.

"Thanks, crew." He nodded at the empty air around the floating china and flatware. Mrs. Redford grinned, then headed out the door to the parlor.

"Yeah, thanks." I finally understood why it wasn't such a big deal for Mrs. Redford to handle a Redcap diet. She had unseen help.

"So, Nox is getting your homework?" Fred reached and grabbed more plates of sandwiches from a counter. He held a bacon, egg, and cheese in one hand and a Reuben in the other.

"Yeah. Well, she's giving most of it to Tony. He's bringing it over here later." I propped one elbow on the table and leaned on my hand.

"Not her?" Fred's eyebrows lifted as he chewed. "Huh."

"Yeah, I know." I swallowed the last of the Velvet Elvis sandwich. "Does anyone know if she's been off campus except for the night she ran into me on Camp Street?"

"Off-campus? It's rare to see her *on* campus unless there's a class." He polished off both sandwiches, then snagged a roast beef and horseradish. "At least, that's the way she was last semester.

Only went to the Nocturnal Lounge for orientation. She's been there practically every night since it got fixed up."

"I wonder why?" I eyed a plate with mostly tuna, egg, and chicken salad sandwiches. Fred grabbed some when he saw I'd passed them up for a turkey with cranberry on wheat.

"Maybe she's taking a lot of classes this Spring." Fred made quick work of the smooshy sandwiches.

"Maybe." I had a feeling that wasn't all. "But she might be hiding." I told Fred about the apparent napping in the cafeteria. "One thing I can't figure, if she's hiding, why would she be out on Camp Street instead of on campus?"

"Depends on who she's hiding from, don't you think?" Invisible hands shuttled empty plates off the table, replacing them with the rest from the counters. Fred inhaled through his nose, smiling when he caught the aroma of steak bomb grinders.

"Oh. You think it's the Sprite thing?" I passed over the grinders, opting for a veal parm panini instead.

"Yeah. I know for sure they're in hiding." Fred polished off the grinders. "Why wouldn't Nox be, too?"

"I hadn't thought of that. But really, what could either Court do to her?" I chewed thoughtfully, relishing the tender texture of the sandwich. "She's not a Changeling who has to pick a side and tithe."

"The magic that lets her shift comes from the Unseelie Court. The King could conscript her and slap her with a punishment." The rest of the pressed sandwiches vanished before Fred continued. "But he probably won't. Dad says he's been in an amazingly good mood since that enchantment got undone. Thinks it's good press for his side, makes Unseelies look like the rule-benders they are instead of creepy evildoers."

"But that's just him, not, um, her." I raised an eyebrow. If the King was cool with letting Nox's transgression slide, the Queen would definitely think the opposite.

"Right." Fred glanced at the half-full plate on the kitchen island. "And good call not saying that name in here. Dad has alarms. Anyway, she'll claim Nox owes her. Probably something big, too."

"That's lame." I tried to hide my shock at the near extinction of edible items. "The Sprite was serving a Summoner. It's not like she could have used them herself until he kicked the bucket or their contract ran out."

"You'd have to talk to Blaine in order to understand that." Fred shrugged. "He's got a much better idea of how virtually immortal people feel about losing things they expect to keep forever."

"Good point." I set my unfinished half panini down on the empty plate in front of me.

"What did Ed say to you upstairs, anyway?" Fred set his elbows on the table, leaning forward.

"He wants me to be more honest." Ironic how my answer halfway ignored the kid's advice.

"Well that's a good idea for anyone, you think?" Fred smirked. I couldn't remember whether Redcaps were any good at detecting lies. Even if they weren't, with a Psychic mom, Fred might have a leg-up on hunches and woojy feelings.

"For most." I nodded. "Not always for an Alpha, or someone hiding from people with excellent senses of smell."

"And that's why it's really for the best that you stayed here." Fred stood, reaching across the table to clap me on one shoulder. "Whole house has glamour on it. They won't smell you here. Unseelies don't dare piss my dad off, and the other Court would get fried if they got within fifty feet of the door."

"Yeah. But I'll have to leave at least once to practice with Nox." I sighed, hoping I didn't sound as Emo as I felt. "Not sure where we'll be able to go that's not on campus and safe for her."

"Someone will think of something." Fred stuffed the last ten sandwiches into a lunchbox in his rucksack. "That's the advantage of having a pack, right? When I get to campus, I'll check with one of your crew."

"Is it that late already?" I also stood, instinctively reaching for my bag before remembering I couldn't go to class all week.

"What do you mean, late?" Fred chuckled. "It's early. This was breakfast."

"Don't tell me you have Second Breakfast and Elevensies, too?" I laughed.

"Hey, no Hobbit meals jokes. Those just go places I don't even want to contemplate." Fred slung the rucksack over one shoulder. "I'll be back later tonight. This is where our Fellowship parts ways."

We laughed, and he left me alone with the remains of my tuna melt on pumpernickel.

CHAPTER FOUR

Nox

I shook off my desire to sleep even though I'd need energy for class later. I couldn't let anyone know I had no place to go. Seelies and Changelings likely to tithe that way went to PPC, but the entire campus was neutral ground. That wouldn't prevent them from following me if I left, however. My apartment didn't have an underground tunnel like Henry's. It wasn't warded because I didn't have enough skill to protect more than a broom closet. Most of my studies had been focused on shifting instead of magic. It's one reason I'd taken Magic Theory 101 as a Junior.

In the ladies' room, the mirrors above the sink gave me bad news. I splashed cold water on my face, hoping to reduce the puffiness under my eyes. At least I wasn't high-maintenance with makeup or hair or anything. That had turned out to be a blessing in disguise while hiding out. This limited wardrobe and bare minimum toiletries thing would have been intolerable for someone like Jeannie the Resident Assistant, or even hair-iron addicted Lynn Frampton. People on campus were used to me looking unkempt, but my weariness was unmistakable now.

I had to find a place to get actual sleep if I wanted to keep my secret and help Josh. I'd checked the Alternative Therapies lab, hoping to find a hospital bed. There was one, but I couldn't risk breaking in. They locked that entire building between classes, and I'd get caught. The dorm basement lounge might still have the air mattress from Henry's stay. I'd just have to find a way to check it out while keeping my homelessness on the down-low.

I headed to the library, remembering how Blaine had mentioned meeting Olivia about an errand. They'd be in there right now. If they had to stop at the dorm before their next class, I could just follow them. A little ice in the lock would hold the main door long enough for me to sneak in later. I walked up the library steps and went inside.

The musty smell of old books and the static crackle of new computers surrounded me. I heard Blaine blathering on about a boat circling the harbor since Christmas, punctuated by Olivia's artificially perky vocalizations of agreement. The owl shifter might be the only person on campus more sleep-deprived than me, but that was her own damn fault. She'd taken meds to go against her natural nocturnal patterns. I wondered why. Extrahuman Law offered courses at all hours. I dismissed the question for the umpteenth time. It was her life and no business of mine unless she decided to share.

Thinking of life got me thinking about Maddie. She was the closest thing to a female friend I had. Lynn was so cerebral, it was hard to talk to her about much besides academics. If she'd been around over the weekend, maybe I could have gotten her help. Umbral magic could hide anyone from most Seelie things unless they watched Maddie casting her spell. But I couldn't expect her to hang around for hours while I slept or chaperon me all over town. I had to keep my big girl pants on and do things for myself.

At least, that's what Grandpa kept twisting my internal arm about, anyway.

My nose wrinkled when I stepped up to the table. Instead of just taking the closest seat, the power of Grandpa compelled me to go all the way around the long table to avoid sitting next to Blaine. He had a beef against the dragon shifter for some reason, maybe even a whole entire cow. I slouched in probably the most uncomfortable chair ever made, nodding at Blaine and Olivia. The corners of my mouth twitched. More battle picking. I let Grandpa stop me from smiling.

"Hi, Nox." Olivia blinked a few times, then rubbed her eyes. When she opened them again, they had unusually large pupils, even for a gal who could turn into an owl. One of my other ancestors, a former doctor, inwardly cringed. I hoped she didn't have a stroke or a heart attack.

I nodded, keeping all the concern to myself. Blaine's lips curled, then parted. His smile was like neon in a 1970s roller rink. I couldn't decide whether he liked me or liked baiting Grandpa even more. Since he studied magic artifacts and anthropology, he had to know a little something about the ancestors all Kelpies and Selkies carried around in their pelts.

Blaine couldn't be old enough to have actually met my grandfather, but his mom might have. Rumor painted Mrs. Harcourt as an honest to goodness warrior princess. Her involvement in stamping out the post-Reveal violence all over Rhode Island only reinforced that reputation. Her son, on the other hand, was a genius-variety entitled brat.

"What's wrong, Nox?" Blaine's voice had a little lilt that let me know a sarcasm bomb was incoming. "Feeling a little hoarse?"

My nostrils flared as I tried to lock myself down and somehow stop the tidal-wave of magical anger Grandpa and all the rest of my ancestors unanimously agreed on unleashing. I stared at a knot in the wooden table in front of me. I imagined roots plunged deep in the soil, siphoning water out, leashing that force to use for nourishment and protection. When the ends of my hair started dripping, I clenched my fist, trying to move my arm across my gut so I could disengage the pelt. No luck. I'd given Grandpa an inch, and he'd taken five hundred miles.

"Miss Phillips, be still." I couldn't place the man's voice even though it was familiar.

The air chilled until icicles brushed my shoulders. I didn't dare turn my head or move. The hair on my arms and the back of my neck stood on end as Grandpa tried to force a shift right there in the library. Across from me, Blaine froze but not with the cold. His wide eyes and hoisted eyebrows meant whoever had me literally on ice was an unexpected visitor to the library. The chair beside me creaked slightly before he spoke again.

"There will be no further outbursts of this nature in my library. Are we clear, Mr. Harcourt?"

"Yes, sir." Blaine folded his hands on the table in front of him, then pulled his arms back as he realized he'd put his elbows on it. Whoever had taken the seat next to me was important enough for Blaine to worry about old-money table manners.

Whatever lowered the temperature eased up enough for me to do more than shiver. I scratched my skin beside my navel when I pulled the pelt free, but that was a small price to pay. I clutched it in one hand, waiting until I could stop my hands from shaking before putting it away in its enchanted oilcloth pouch. That had been a close call. You could get expelled for shifting indoors.

"You will apologize to Miss Phillips and then leave with your minion, Mr. Harcourt." The voice was formal but lacked the stern edge it carried earlier.

"Sorry, Nox." The left corner of Blaine's mouth tilted up, an unconscious signal of insincerity.

"You will do better than that." The voice chilled down to absolute zero.

"I apologize, Miss Phillips. It won't happen again." Blaine

collected his jacket and backpack, then backed away, bowing slightly at the waist. He glanced nervously at Olivia. "Um, let's go to one of the dorm lounges, Olivia, okay?"

"Oh. Okay." Olivia bolted up from her seat like she'd had seven shots of intravenous espresso. "Hoo boy," she said over her shoulder. They left the library like a flight of arrows.

"Thank you, sir." I turned in my seat, giving the distinguished-looking man next to me a little bow like Blaine had. I wasn't sure who or what he was, but Blaine's best behavior was a good template for formality with the elderly fellow.

"If only the young men on campus acted with half the decorum of the young women, you'd have no need to thank me." His smile made his eyes twinkle like chips of obsidian embedded in terra-cotta clay. "I'm Taki Waban. Headmistress Thurston asked me to care for this library now that it's been rebuilt."

"Well, I think you're doing a wonderful job so far, Mr. Waban." I couldn't find my smile. Something about the new librarian was profoundly unsettling even though he looked like a harmless little man of Indigenous heritage. He carried a weight of ages that didn't match even his apparent fifty-something appearance.

"Do you, really? My talents lie less with tomes and more with confounding trouble though I suppose you could call me a book-worm." Something between a chuckle and a rumble rattled in his throat as though he had bronchitis. "Miss Frampton insists quite adamantly that the stacks are organized like a—" He tilted his head. "How does she put it? Ah yes, like a nerf-herder stampede handled the shelving." His lips tilted up in a trace of a smile.

"She doesn't take well to change." I felt most of the tension leave my no-longer-shivering shoulders. He had master-level control of his magic if he'd frozen my pelt's water and cut it back that fast. But he seemed friendly enough to me.

"Unlike some of her cohorts." He indicated me with a flat hand, palm up. "I'll be blunt. Miss Phillips, your will is stronger than the iron that bans your kind, but even you need to sleep sometime."

"I know, sir." I glanced at the door, realizing there was no one to follow into the dorm. "It's just that, besides the Lounge, I haven't got anywhere to go." My eyes stung, whether from lack of sleep or because, once spoken, the fact finally had the power to wound me.

"I understand your predicament all too well." He nodded. "That's why I always carry some of these. I have some spares. Take them." He held out his other hand, revealing a trio of what looked like lead crystal keys. They flickered blue even in the yellow incandescent light of the library. I recognized them immediately, even without the magic sight of my pelt.

"Church-keys? You really want to give that many of these away?" This kind of church-key didn't open beer bottles. Instead, they turned the space behind ordinary doors into heavily warded panic rooms. I'd have to bring something to sleep on every time, but what Mr. Waban offered were three chances at absolute safety for as long as I needed. I wondered how he'd got so many. They could only be made from ice dragon tears.

"They aren't mine to give." He placed them on the table in front of me. "They're yours, Miss Phillips. I've only been holding on to them for you."

"I don't know how to thank you." I pressed the palms of my hands flat against the table, not even daring to hope this wasn't some kind of weird joke.

"Use one of them today. I'll consider that sufficient thanks." The corners of his eyes crinkled again.

"But sir, what do I owe you? You've held onto them all this time." My gaze dropped down to the glimmering keys on the table. My hope was tarnished around the edges with unexpected guilt.

"Nothing. That price was paid before you were born." His voice lowered, whether from a desire for secrecy or sadness, I'd never know. I couldn't bring myself to look back up at him, meet that jet gaze.

"Oh." My exhausted mind couldn't make sense of his statement, only the fact that I didn't owe him anything. "Well, I'll go and use one, then, like you said. Thanks again, Mr. Waban." I stood, only realizing then that I hadn't even bothered to put down the extra-large bag I'd been lugging around with me. I headed toward the narrow hall leading to the stairwell. Pocketing two of the keys, I pointed the third at the door to a broom closet.

It opened on a bare room, narrow but long and wide enough for me to lie down comfortably with my things. There was even space for me to take off my shoes and jacket. I set the alarm on my phone, surprised that it had three bars in here. I lay on my back, hands laced under my head. After that, I couldn't do anything besides fall asleep.

CHAPTER FIVE

Josh

I was up to my elbows in homework on Wednesday night when Fred showed up with Maddie. They checked over every corner of the room I'd been staying in, making sure there weren't any spy devices like there'd been in the Nocturnal Lounge. Then, Fred pulled down the window shade and closed the curtains. Maddie called up her magic, gathering shadows around the both of us. I'd seen her do it before when she'd hidden herself and Nox outside Professor Brodsky's apartment. Being in the shadows was way different. I wondered why Nox hadn't mentioned how weird it was, seeing everything in muted purple hues. Then again, I'd tried to avoid her.

"Okay, Maddie. Follow me out. I'll get the mail. You just go over to that place Olivia showed you earlier." Fred opened the door and headed into the hall.

Maddie was too smart to answer. Clearly they'd already discussed the plan earlier. I was just along for the ride, so I went with it. That felt natural, unfortunately. How was I supposed to head up two powerful packs in the future if I kept letting myself get dragged along by Magi and Redcaps and bears, oh my?

Maddie walked fast for such a short girl. She beat feet like a champion power-walker, heading all the way down College Hill to North Main Street. On the corner outside RISD, we passed some hipsters. I would have loved to pop out at them, shock them out of their blasé broken-hip hangout poses. Too dangerous. Henry had already pranked the lumbersexuals and the shabby chics this way.

Maddie took a right and headed up the street. A few blocks later, Maddie stopped in front of a dojo. The sign up top was red with little pink flowers and the words Cherry Blossom School. A kanji I assumed to be a translation squatted beside the English lettering. Maddie stood at the door, waiting. I sighed, wishing for a fraction of the patience she seemed to possess. After what seemed like an hour but was probably more like sixty seconds, the door opened.

A stream of kids, mostly in the awkward 'tween age-bracket, trotted out. Their pimply little faces wore smiles for the most part. I almost missed slipping through the door as I watched them hop into waiting cars or shuffle toward their expectant adult counterparts. I made it through thanks to a sharp gust of cold wind slowing the door's trajectory. Once it closed behind us, Maddie relaxed, releasing her shadow magic.

"Less lollygagging on the way home, Josh," Maddie ordered, tapping one small foot on the linoleum. "We wouldn't have made it here on time for the class to let out otherwise. And we need to get you back to Fred's in time for his mom to let the cat out."

"Wait, an actual cat?" I scratched my head. "I haven't seen one the entire time I've been there."

"No, Tony." She smiled. "He'll be heading out after he swaps your homework."

"Oh. Okay, then." I looked around. Trophies lined the shelves in front of whitewashed wood-paneled walls. The wall behind the small reception counter held framed teaching credentials, some Extrahuman. The space was unfamiliar, but the trophies reminded me of something. I hadn't been to this martial arts school before, but Beth's dead beau had run one on the other side of town. I shivered for no good reason. "Where's Nox?"

"I brought her over before I got you. She said to just head on in there." Maddie waved her hand, sitting with her back to the wall between the practice space and waiting room, facing the street entrance. "I've got reading to do while you two spar. Have fun." The coy little smile the Umbral magus gave me was the first sign that strange things were afoot at the Cherry Blossom School.

I stepped through the bisected black and white flag that served as a door. At a glance, it seemed empty. The faint shimmer in one corner told me otherwise. Even if I hadn't seen that, the low, mossy scent of a pond during a thunderstorm gave her away. I headed straight for the corner with the shimmer, lunging at the approximate height of Nox's waist.

I got an arm full of nothing and a face-full of wall when she swept my leg. Blood dripped from my nose, landing on a gray scarf I'd last seen draped around Nox's neck. I sold more pain than her unexpected attack actually caused, trying to fake her out. Fail city. She caught me by the upper arm as I staggered away from her. I found myself looking at the drop-ceiling just a moment later.

I kipped up, ducking out of the way of the left hook she'd aimed at my already healed nose. Nox or one of her ancestors must have fought wolf shifters before. Going for the nose gave any opponent with glamour or cloaking an advantage since we relied on scent for accuracy. I kept my chin tucked, darting past her almost all the way back to the flag-draped door. She outpaced me. I should have expected a faerie horse shifter to be speedier than Gonzales.

I spun on my heel, aiming an uppercut at her chin. It

connected, throwing her off balance. Her wobbly attempt at steadying herself gave me time to get behind her and grapple her under her arms. I thought I had her, but the wet, mossy scent intensified and her skin got all slippery. How she perspired that much in a chilly dojo was beyond me until I realized it was water magic. I tried to hold on, wrapping my hands in the damp fabric of her shirt.

We staggered halfway across the room together in what could have been some kind of post-modern interpretive dance-fight. I pushed against her back as hard as I could, trying to get her on the ground. Thoughts that had nothing at all to do with sparring flashed through my head, a completely inappropriate set of carnal images transmitted by my wolf. I banished them from my mind, but couldn't do a damn thing about my body. It seemed to distract her, at least. Nox's knees buckled, making me think I'd won. But then, the sound of tearing fabric told me I got served.

I ended up on my back again but didn't dare kip up this time. My hands were in the indecipherable tangle of the tattered remains of Nox's tank top. She had the whole mess pinned to the floor above my head. Her thigh was in an extremely inconvenient location, too. It felt like my face caught fire when I glanced down to see flashes of pale skin through the black lace of her bra. A chuckle halfway between a whicker and running water sounded in my left ear, and a low, velvety growl joined it. My wolf wasn't nearly as embarrassed with this round's outcome as I'd been.

"Someone likes a good match." Nox let go of my hands, smiling down at me. She licked her lips then shook her head, sending drops of water out in a nimbus.

"More than one someone." I brought my hands down, glad to have the torn shirt to deal with so I didn't have to get up right away. Not that I had any illusions that Nox hadn't noticed the state I was in.

"Wow. You borrowed that ego from Blaine?" Nox stood, turning her back to me as she headed over to a huge rucksack I hadn't noticed by the scarf. She got out a white tank and pulled it over her head. Shouldn't have bothered. It got soaked through in moments. The bra was even more distracting now.

"What?" I sat up, still failing miserably in my effort not to ogle her. "Ego?"

"You just go ahead and—" Nox let out a low grunt of effort. "Of course. You meant you and your wolf. And there I went, about to accuse you of assuming something." She turned around again, her face relaxed except for one line between her eyebrows. "Sorry for the outburst, Josh. Not for wiping the floor with you. That was fun."

"Fun?" I untangled my hands, then used them to spike up my hair. "That's all I am to you?" I winked to cover for my inside voice getting out. Maybe she'd think it was a joke.

"Maybe." She put her hands on her hips. "Want to go again?"

"No Glamour this time." I could have asked instead of ordered, but dammit, I was her Alpha, even though our pack was strictly of the rinky-dink variety.

"Why not?" She raised an eyebrow, pursing her lips. They glistened like the rest of her. I wasn't sure I'd be able to find another woman attractive again after that. Nox Phillips was ruining me just by standing there, waiting for an answer.

"No one in the class I'm practicing for can do that." I had to clear my throat, grateful my voice hadn't actually cracked like a lame teenager.

"Hmm." She put her hands together, lacing her fingers and cracking her knuckles. "Okay. We'll do it your way this time."

I just nodded. Either Nox didn't care that my family had to stay impartial, or she was using banter as a distraction. There was no way she didn't know nothing should happen between us. A couple of months ago, I'd have just assumed she just wanted to jump my bones. After the whole business over Winter Break, I'd never think something like that about Nox Phillips. She was a fighter, not a lover. She shut down unwanted flirting more handily than she'd just trounced me.

We circled the middle of the room, facing each other, stances combat-ready. I watched her eyes like every fight coach worth his salt had told me. Nox did no such thing. She stared just above the space between my eyes. It was unfamiliar, unsettling too. She'd already bested me once that night. I shouldn't let it happen again but had no idea what she was up to.

It felt like stalemate city the way we both held our ground. My patience ran out, the wolf inside making the biggest racket in the universe as it urged me to go ahead and grab her. I clenched my jaw, held my wolf by the throat, pushed it down. Raw ferocity would do nothing for me here even if my wolf had something on its mind besides fighting.

Nox leaped forward, full center. No faking one way or the other for her. Her arm came up at the last second, clunking me in the chin. If my jaw hadn't been clenched, I might have bitten the tip of my tongue. The blow knocked me back, but not over. I noticed she'd lifted her chin, so I went for her throat with my hands. My wolf, riled up at being held down all that time, had other ideas.

I ran her to the wall, one hand on her neck and the other clamped on her shoulder. Nox gasped as my mouth met her throat, teeth grazing her flesh. Despite her flirtatious talk earlier, she reacted to it like a threat instead of a come-on. Definitely a fighter. I wasn't entirely sure which I'd meant myself and she gave me no time to figure it out.

Nox used magic again, making me kick myself for not banning that, too. My mouth filled with water so cold it could have come off a glacier. I had to let go and spit it out or risk it going up my nose and cutting off my air. She managed to get her hands around my wrists, pushing against me as she tried to break my grasp. Then, the lights purpled and went out.

A rustle of fabric and an icy breeze told me someone had

come through the front entrance. The lights came on again along with the sound of one footstep and a puzzlingly familiar dragging sound. Nox and I broke it up, both turning toward the flag covering the doorway.

"Oh—" Maddie sounded like someone who'd just seen an injured animal. Her footsteps joined the visitor's. Moments later, the flag parted to reveal who'd interrupted our practice.

"Beth!" I rushed forward to help my sister as she hobbled forward on her remaining leg and a rickety wooden crutch.

"Josh." She sighed like the last autumn leaf dropping to the ground. Her knee buckled. "Never thought I'd find you. 'Specially not here."

"How did you get away?" I let her lean on me, led her back through the curtain to settle her on a chair next to Maddie.

"I didn't. They let me go." She tried to prop the crutch against the wall, but it slid sideways. Beth looked like she was near tears until Nox caught and righted it. "Thanks."

"Wait. Without your prosthetic?" I knelt on the floor in front of my formerly reclusive sister. "Who do I have to kill?"

"Uncle Jake." She leaned her elbows on her thighs, resting her head on her hands. That's how she used to sit in the tree fort back when we were kids. My heart nearly split open with rage.

"Son of a bitch." I made a fist, about to ventilate the wall with it. Nox stopped it with a palm. Something crunched, pain flashing in my knuckles, but it'd heal in a minute. "I should have known." Jake was Mom's brother. He'd always been pissed that she hadn't given him her pack once she married Dad.

"Yes, you should have." Beth peered up at me through damp eyelashes, a muscle in her jaw twitching. My sister always got teary when she was angry. But why'd she direct it at me?

"So this is somehow my fault?" I paced toward the desk, then back again.

"Not completely." Beth shook her head. "But it's your responsibility. You're the heir."

"Funny how that goes, isn't it?" I ran a hand through my hair.

"I didn't want this either, you know." She glanced at the spot where her right knee should be.

"Yeah, I know." The accident hadn't been her fault, or Ren's. Drunk drivers suck. Missing older brothers suck, too.

"It's weird being here." Beth shook her head at the wall behind the counter. "Seeing him again."

I followed her gaze. I'd been so focused on meeting Nox, I hadn't checked the name on all the credentials, or the small photo far to the right and at the bottom of the display space. Ichiro. Ren's father hadn't shut down the dojo. He'd just renamed and moved it. I looked up at the trophies on the other wall. The three biggest had the name Phillips on them. No wonder I hadn't been able to beat Nox. Small world.

"Yeah, weird." I sighed, trying to focus. "So they let you go. Why?" Since that damned accident, talking to my sister was like pulling teeth sometimes.

"Got a message to give you." Beth reached into her jacket, rummaging in the interior pocket. "Here. I'm not sure what it says."

I broke the seal, trying not to look surprised that it was formally addressed and composed like a letter to the Alpha of a rival pack. Nox read it over my shoulder. I couldn't figure out why Uncle Jake would bother with this level of formality. I hadn't inherited my place at the head of either of my parents' packs yet. I leaned back, feeling the weight of my half of the alliance medallion tap me on the breastbone.

"Oh." My right hand flew to my chest, clutching the metallic object along with the fabric covering it. "They wanted me, not you guys. Tinfoil Hat's more important than I thought."

"You're so dense sometimes." Beth shook her head. "I mean, really? You think they didn't want you as bad as they wanted our folks after you went and made a vampire your Beta?"

"Yeah, well, they didn't get me on the New Moon." I turned the letter around so she could see it. "Sucks to be them."

"That alliance makes you a real Alpha." Nox slapped me on the shoulder. "Good for you. Not so good for me."

"We'll figure something out." I blinked, not daring to even look at Nox. I tried not to notice Beth staring at me like I'd suddenly turned green or something. "My Uncle can try to negotiate a prisoner exchange, but since I'm a real Alpha, I can fight him instead."

"But it's not Uncle Jake and company who want her." Beth pointed to some fine print below the second signature line. "He must owe something big. Do you see who witnessed this?"

"Oh, no." Maddie gulped.

"Yeah, well." Nox snorted. "You piss off the Sidhe Queen enough, she gets involved. When's this happening?"

"Half-moon." Beth looked at Nox, then at me. She sighed. "That's Monday."

"And things will just get more dangerous for me after that. She's more powerful when the moon's on the wax." Nox crossed her arms over her chest. "Maybe I should just agree to stand trial."

"Do you get a lawyer in Faerie trials?" Maddie stood up, stepping next to her friend. She didn't touch Nox, though.

"Yeah, but only for sentencing. Guilt's determined by magic. I definitely did it, nothing will say otherwise. No Faerie will touch this. Probably not any other Extrahuman lawyer, either."

"We'll think of something." Maddie tapped her chin with one finger. "Maybe Olivia…hmm. But she's just a student, not even interning until summer." She scratched her head.

"You need to think of nothing as far as legal issues go." I jumped up at the unexpected voice. Beth covered her mouth. Maddie turned. Nox's shoulders straightened. "I will represent you."

"Ichiro-San." She bowed at the waist. "Thank you."

"Thank me when your trial is complete." The middle-aged man who'd walked through a hidden door behind the counter peered at each of us in turn. "I'm more than qualified to plead your case. And as you know, I've got an extra advantage. Luck will be on your side." He winked at Nox, and she smiled nearly as widely as she had the night she'd found me wandering the streets in my pajamas.

"What's he mean?" Maddie blinked, then squinted at Mr. Ichiro. I already knew, of course. So did Beth. I kept my mouth shut to let Nox tell her friend the awesome news.

"Ichiro-san isn't just the owner of Cherry Blossom School or a lawyer. He's a Tanuki."

CHAPTER SIX

Nox

Grandpa's happiness at Ichiro-san's offer had me so pumped up I barely noticed Beth put her head in her hands. A keening so high pitched it was almost inaudible came from between her palms. I tried to batter down the solid wall of gloating that came from him and the rest of my ancestors but barely made a dent.

Ichiro-san went straight to Beth just as I finally realized why Josh's last name had seemed so familiar when we'd met. It had been in the obituary my last year of High School. Ren Ichiro, survived by his father, sister, and fiancée Beth Dennison. I glanced away from the stump of her leg, thankful my grandfather had seen worse and didn't want to stare. She'd lost her mate and her leg. No wonder Josh had to be Alpha. Losing Ren was probably worse for her than losing the limb. Wolf shifters got unstable and volatile without a mate, sometimes needing to be locked up by their packs. Beth might be able to find another fellow. Coincidence wasn't so cruel as to only have one potential mate in the world for each person. But she didn't seem like she wanted to look even after three years.

Josh was by the counter, checking out the hidden door. I knew about it but had never actually seen it. His fists clenched, posture stiffening. I watched the back of his neck redden as I approached him. Grandpa wouldn't be happy if I did anything to comfort him physically, so I just walked near enough to brush his shoulder with mine.

"Did you know he could see us that whole time, Nox?" Josh jerked his chin at a bank of glass inside the narrow room. One-way mirror, of course.

"No. Is the fact that he did going to be a problem?" I felt my cheeks heat up as I realized my late sensei's dad had seen me shirtless and using a sparring match as a crude form of flirtation.

"Luna's Light." He let out his remaining breath slowly. "I shouldn't let it be. Yeah, that'd be for the best. Not a problem."

"I'm glad." I took a step away, but Josh caught me by the arm. "But I didn't mean—"

"Listen." His whisper carried a hint of a growl. "I don't know what your deal is, but I'm letting the fact that he saw you beat me slide for my sister. You will tell me what this is all about later. Understand?"

"Perfectly." I turned my head, not having to tilt it down to look him in the eye. His usually honey-brown eyes brightened to a yellow-amber color. I put one hand over my stomach, gasping as I pulled my pelt free. "I'll explain. I couldn't with this thing on and now is definitely not the time."

"When, then?" Josh's eyebrows slanted frown-ward as his eyes narrowed. "Seems like there'll be none with classes and trials."

"I don't know." I shrugged, my fist tightening on the slippery pelt. "If it's important to you, then make time."

"Swan Point. Memorial Grove." The reason for his choice stung my eyes with threatening tears. Ren Ichiro's body had never been found, and Josh's brother was also presumed dead.

The Grove was a place to mourn those who'd never come home. Like my father.

"The Megalith?" I wanted to shut my eyes, but couldn't. The giant stone had been brought over from South County back before the Big Reveal. I'd been there every year since Dad died, but he still hadn't moved on.

"Yeah. Midnight work for you?" Josh's eyebrows went back to their usual level.

"I'll make it." I nodded. This time, when I pulled away, he let me go. It'd take a covert effort to get over there, but our entire situation had gotten loads more complicated. Refusing to talk about what might be between us would be the height of idiocy.

I heard Ichiro-San call a cab for Beth. I sighed, worried I'd be on my own on the way back to campus. The old Tanuki would want to get Beth somewhere safe immediately. His ability to choose the luckiest route wouldn't be available to me, and Maddie would need to bring Josh back to Fred's. But she surprised me by linking her arm through mine.

"Mr. Ichiro will bring Josh with him. It's okay. They can't nab him now that it's not the New Moon, anyway." She glanced at Beth, who nodded.

"Yeah, they said he's off-limits. Made it abundantly clear they think that's only temporary." She looked so tired, I wanted to give her a hug. Almost. Beth's inability to get over losing Ren only made things more difficult for Josh. I softened. It wasn't right to judge her about losing her mate when I didn't even know what it was like to have one .

I took a deep breath, watching Mr. Ichiro help Beth from her seat to the door, Josh following closely. Maddie had already drawn her shadows around us, so we followed them out. As my head cleared, I wondered why Josh's troubles were such a big deal to me, anyway.

"You're super protective of him suddenly, huh?" Maddie glanced at me as we walked arm-in-arm up the street.

"Um." My teeth squeaked as I clenched my jaw. "Him who?"

"Oh, come on, Nox." Maddie shook her head, making her curls bounce. I couldn't get mad at her. She was just being a friend.

"Yeah, Maddie. Fine." I rolled my eyes. "Josh is driving me batty. I can't make any sense of how he acts around me, mostly because I can barely think straight around him. I don't know if I want to kick him or kiss him half the time."

"Well, I think he likes you." She grinned. "Maybe you two should give things a shot."

"At least you getting together with Henry didn't start a war." I sighed. Maddie's dad was a vampire, and her mom had had a license to get turned. They were happy for her as long as she finished school before applying for a license of her own.

"You really think that's where this is headed?" She patted my arm with one brown hand. "War between who?"

"If the trial was just his uncle trying to take over, then maybe not." We walked another half a block up the hill before I spoke again. "But it looks like Josh and I screwed something up when we helped you guys over winter break. His uncle might just be trying to fix things. The way Beth talked about the Queen getting involved almost seems like she had a hand in their pack politics. Or maybe someone else did."

"But why?" Maddie's curls bounced as she shook her head. "If the Queen has a problem with you, why would she involve the Dennisons?"

"Maybe she wants to work through someone else at this time of year. And maybe she didn't, like I said. She might just have seen the pack problem and decide to use it to her advantage." I listened to her boots and my sneakers tap and squeak against the damp pavement. "If she lets Unseelies get away with stuff like what I did, the Seelies will lose power. She can't afford that."

"Sounds like a big mess." Maddie stopped, tugging on my arm.

We'd gotten to Thayer Street. "Want me to have the Tinfoil Hat brainiac society look at it?"

"They can try." I tugged back, urging her to keep on walking with me. "There's not going to be much for them to go on until we know what she's aiming to sentence me with."

"Make me a list of possibilities. I'll get Lynn and Blaine in on it with me." She chuckled. "Lynn says they read at warp factor nine."

I actually laughed but remembered to keep it quiet enough not to break out of the shadow magic she'd hidden us with. We turned down toward the Thayer Trolley Tunnel, where I did the special knock to open the secret door. Maddie said goodbye at the bottom of the stairs to go finish her homework. Once through the doorway, I was on campus and safe. The Nocturnal Lounge was emptier than usual. Checking a flier on the wall by the coffee and snack station told me why. Night Creatures were playing down at The Living Room. The usual crowd here would all be over there supporting them. I sighed, sinking into one of the new-to-PPC cushy chairs, relishing some alone time. Maybe I could even take a short snooze.

The clunk and tap of worn boot-heels told me I wasn't completely alone. I sat up, turning most of the way around in my seat to find Bianca the Psychic Medium smiling at me. She grabbed a cup of tea as she came , the bag tag fluttering in the breeze of her passage like a tiny moth around a flame. Except that when she sat down and set the cup on the end table next to her, the tag just kept on flapping.

"You look atypically mournful tonight." Bianca didn't usually notice the living too much unless the place was empty like now, or they seemed down in the dumps. She twirled some of her pink-tipped blonde hair between her fingers absently.

"Yeah. Got a lot to think about." I rubbed my eyes. "Not enough time as I'd like, either."

Most people would have taken my words as a strong hint to

just get lost already, but not Bianca. She didn't have much people sense unless the people in question weren't exactly in this world anymore. It had to be odd, seeing an entire city full of ghosts when no one else could. Weird enough to make her weird, too. Then again, maybe it took an already out-of-touch person to make the kind of contact Mediums could with the Other Side. I decided to let my overtired mind drop the whole idea like the chicken and egg argument it seemed to be. Regardless, Mediums kept ghosts from freaking out. Most people appreciated them, but usually from afar to avoid the flakiness that went with talking to invisible dead people.

"Well, I'd leave you to it, but if I did, he wouldn't leave me alone." Bianca glanced at the fluttering tea tag. "Horace, that is. Usually, he's a great ghost to have around." Her usually vacantly kind face took on an expression that would have looked more at home on Headmistress Thurston. "Tonight, he's being an absolute pest because there's something you need to know about your ancestors."

"So what's Horace on about then?" I figured handling this situation with Grandpa's ornery abruptness might be for the best.

"Well, he says your father's been bothering him. Keeps going on about how your grandpa makes you deny everything, whatever that means."

"Wait, what?" I blinked, leaning forward. "No way Dad's here."

"Oh, of course, he's not. He's contracted down at the Reservoir like he's supposed to be. But part of Horace's job is to go around and check on ghostly workers all over the state." Bianca rolled her eyes in the direction of her tea. "And that's how your father gave him an earful. He's so agitated, it's causing problems with the piping at the water treatment plant."

"So, Horace." I set my gaze vaguely at the spot Bianca had looked at. "What's my dad's problem, anyway?"

Bianca smiled. She nodded at the empty space as though listening to something.

"Horace says thanks for talking to him instead of me. He also says your dad's worried you're ruining your chances of finding your mate. Something about listening to your heart instead of your grandfather, whatever that means."

"And how would he know, anyway?" I slapped a hand over my mouth. "Ugh. That was supposed to be my inside voice."

"Why not have a nice cup of peppermint or chamomile tea and then relax?" Bianca's eyebrows made light-brown arcs. "You seem like you're on edge. No wonder your dad's worried about you."

"Bianca, I know you and Horace mean well, but you have no idea." I shook my head. "The last thing I need right now was a scolding from the hereafter that doesn't make any sense."

"Sorry if that message is unclear." Bianca turned, glancing at where the tea bag tag fluttered against the side of the cup even more rapidly. "What's that, Horace?" She made her listening face again, this time with extra forehead crinkle. "Huh."

"What is it now?" I glanced between her and where I thought the ghost was.

"Okay. He wants me to tell you that your dad knows what he's talking about. Your grandpa's going to get you in trouble. Horace says to remember how strong his influence is. You need to make peace with him, or you might lose part of yourself."

"What is Horace anyway, a ghostly Precog?" I raised an eyebrow. Precog ghosts were rare. Since most of them saw their own death coming, they'd usually finish any business before death.

"No. He's a Ghostly Medium, my mentor since I almost died." Bianca sighed. "Look, all I know myself is, your dad must have been upset. There was worry ectoplasm all around Horace when he came back from the reservoir."

"This is pretty confusing for me." I shook my head. "We don't take anything but Psychic Ways 101 in my major."

"Sorry, Nox. We tried to make it simple. The main thing I guess is, your dad wants you to be happy. He's worried you're about to walk into a situation where that won't happen if you don't stand up for yourself. Something about coincidence."

"Gah, not coincidence again." I ran my hands through my hair. "At least that's something I understand, though. Look, Bianca. Thanks for the chat. And thanks, Horace, for the information. I'm just not sure there's much I can do with it."

"Yeah, I kind of figured." Bianca stood up and reached into the hammock-shaped tie-dye bag she always carried. "Have some of these. They're better than tea when things get really rough." She dropped a few foil-wrapped packages on the table next to me. Then, she collected her cup. "Come on, Horace. We've got library ghosts to check in on."

"Thanks." When she turned at the top of the stairs to flap a hand in farewell, I waved back.

The packages were chocolates, so dark milk or cream couldn't have been within miles of the factory that made them. I bit into one, the bittersweet taste reminding me of my meeting and that load of explaining to do. If only any of this made sense.

Grandpa was always a troublemaker. I'd never realized how much until Dad died protesting water privatization and I inherited the pelt that made me a Kelpie. I wasn't sure I'd be able to stand up to Grandpa without Dad's help. But until his ghost moved on, the part of him that belonged to the pelt was stuck in limbo. I wondered whether helping Dad finish his business would help me with the Old Boy's Club I had to handle every time I put my pelt on.

But what was Dad's unfinished business? That's what I should have asked Horace. I grabbed another chocolate, frowning at my failure to think of such an obvious question. As the candy melted slowly in my mouth, I sighed. I shouldn't beat myself up over it.

I'd had maybe six hours of sleep in as many days. His unfinished business had to have something to do with me. If I really wanted to know, there was one way I might find out.

I pulled my phone from my rucksack, tapped it out of sleep and swiped away the screen-saver. My finger hovered over the dial button next to the entry marked Mom. I hadn't heard her voice since the middle of summer when she made her annual trip to Block Island. After Dad died and my brother Uri moved out, she'd sold everything and moved to Key West. It was always islands with her. My brother and I had done nothing but disappoint her, neither of us inheriting her Water magic.

She'd never made her feelings secret but didn't use them against either of us like she could have. Mom was a sour woman, but self-aware. She kept her distance instead of unleashing a torrent of abuse like some other people might have. I tapped the yellow text icon instead of the green call one.

Dad have any unfinished business I should know about? I set the phone next to the last piece of chocolate and got up to fix some coffee instead of the tea Bianca suggested. It looked like I wasn't going to get that nap after all, so it was caffeine jitters time for me. I tapped one foot, stirring cream in the coffee. I didn't understand how Maddie could put so much sugar in hers. Light and bitter was my constant coffee order. After one sip, I sat back in the chair to wait. Less than a minute later, I got my mother's blunt reply.

You. He always wanted to see you happy. Find your mate, and he'll move on. I waited to reply, absolutely sure I didn't want to play one of her blame games while sleep-deprived.

Thanks, Mom. It was the only safe reply. Still, she wasn't about to leave it at that.

Find and accept. Why ask this now? I glared at the words. It'd take too long to tell, and the last thing I wanted was Mom involving herself in this. She'd help, but do it while looking down her nose the entire time. If I didn't answer, she'd call. I wasn't sure I could handle that in crisis mode.

Busybody Psychic. It felt wrong to throw Bianca under the bus like that, especially after she'd given me chocolate. I could apologize to her some other time. There was no question it'd get back to her. The skeleton crew loved her, and any of them could read my texts.

Is there a boy? Even though I'd turn twenty-one in the summer, Mom still talked to me about boys instead of men.

Maybe.

Complicated?

A little bit.

You'll handle it, you're a big girl. Night, Nox.

I sent back a similar sentiment, glad the conversation was over. I closed out of the messaging screen, revealing the time. Was it really eleven already? I'd have to head out now to make it to Swan Point in time. I pulled the oilcloth bag from my pack, glad I could shift with it. Only magical shifters could take something with them. I chose the woolen blanket in my rucksack, tying it around me in what I hoped was a modest enough fashion. I undressed under it, thankful I had water magic to warm me the whole way. Shoes were out of the question, and I had a long tunnel to traverse before I could shift.

I pressed the pelt against my bare stomach until it melded with the skin there, then tucked the pouch between two of the knots holding my improvised dress together. Why we couldn't have met on campus had me baffled until I stowed my things in one of the lockers under the emergency sun blankets.

I stared at the Campus Police logo. Who'd been running the department since Josh's dad had been detained? He must want to keep the details of our conversation out of their ears. I engaged the combination lock, then headed through the underground door, raising a bubble of glamour around myself as I stepped through. Unseelies would be able to see through it, but only a traitor would report me to the Seelies. I let muscle memory and instinct lead me toward fresh water. Then, I settled in for what I hoped would be a productive internal conversation. I sighed, remembering that quote of Albus Dumbledore's. "Of course it is happening inside your head, Harry, but why on earth should that mean that it is not real?"

Grandpa, what's your problem? He piped up right away.

You know. I expected a boy. Phillips Kelpies are always boys. You make all this more difficult than it should be. I got an impression of shaggy salt-white hair atop a grizzled face, an untidy contrast to the photographs that always showed him clean-shaven. I realized he mustn't have had time to clean himself up before he died.

So blame Uri for getting Earth magic. I am what I am. Are you sure you're not the one making this difficult? I can't change, and it's either me or get locked up in a vault or a hoard.

We might as well have been stored for the next generation. Everyone behind me thinks you won't be brave enough to do what has to be done. Images of tall men dying in combat flickered through my mind.

Times are different now. We're not secret anymore. And how dare you imply I'm not brave? I projected my own image of the morning I removed the Sidhe Queen's magic from a poor, tormented creature.

You're admirably defiant, we'll give you that. But we're not convinced you're capable of sacrifice. Your rebellious streak is part of the problem. All you do is fight us when we're the ones who really know what being a Kelpie is all about. This time, he showed me placid lake shorelines, pristine riversides, ponds kept safe from the ravages of the modern age.

You're angry that I'm not Greenpeace Eco-Warrior enough? That's your big issue? I shook my head.

The King gave us our magic so we could protect these places, not so we could anger his Queen. They were in love then, remember? You need to start applying yourself to those ends. Make amends to her. His face in my mind's eye suddenly looked more tired than I felt. *And get rid of the idea I'm so hidebound that I can't understand modern sacrifice will look different from what it was in my day.*

Okay, Grandpa. Can we stop fighting each other so much of the time now? I sighed, startling myself as the sound echoed against water at the end of the tunnel. I'd come to the place where I could shift.

One more thing, and we'll try to settle down. Your mate.

I don't have one yet, remember? I stepped to the water's edge, letting my toes touch the rime of ice where it met the pavement.

Resolve that as soon as you can. This time, the voice coming through my mind was smoother and heavily accented with nasal vowels. *Time is short. We need your father here.* The impression of this ancestor's face was bleary with time, but still recognizable as my great-great-great-grandfather. He'd been born a Precognitive psychic.

Working on that. I visualized Josh. *Stop fighting me on it.* The sounds of eleven different laughs mingled in my mind's ear, finally resolving into words spoken in near-perfect unison.

Silly girl. We weren't fighting you. We've been testing him. The voices of my ancestors mingled and faded as my arms and legs elongated. My neck thickened and lengthened. The wool blanket became a piebald marking across my back. I stepped into the water, ducking under as I swam out of the tunnel and upstream toward Swan Point Cemetery.

CHAPTER SEVEN

Josh

Most of the way to the Ichiro house on Angell Street, Beth stared out the window. I didn't blame her. The grubbiness of her face, hair, and clothes plus her missing prosthetic equaled neglect wherever she'd been kept. Having to track me on one rickety crutch all the way to her dead mate's dojo must have made it even worse. And now, she'd have to spend the rest of the time until Monday at his father's house. This sucked more for her than it did for me.

I watched her for a while, hoping maybe all these straws would break the back of my sister's depression camel. No such luck, even while riding in a cab next to a Tanuki. They were luck-masters. People had been shocked when Ren Ichiro vanished into Narragansett Bay, never to be seen again. I hadn't. I'd watched their courtship. Ren hadn't inherited his dad's powers. He'd just had a general magic affinity, able to sense and activate devices like a psychic could. Still, people thought he should have lived.

He'd been popular in the community, way more so than Beth. The public reactions to his death had been almost as bad for her as losing him. Some people even blamed her.

The old lawyer caught me looking. He gave me a wan smile, shaking his head slightly. I swallowed my sigh. I couldn't help Beth. All I could do was wish her well and hope she helped herself one of these days.

Mr. Ichiro had painted the house white since the last time I'd been there. The shutters were still the same light gray they'd been when the siding was red. But now, the entire place looked like bleached bone under the orange glare of an old sodium lamp that still hadn't been replaced with LEDs. Hairs on the back of my neck stood up as we got out of the car. Something wasn't right at the house.

Mr. Ichiro made me and Beth wait on the sidewalk as the cab pulled away. The way he left us made me think I should be on guard though nothing smelled out of the ordinary for a Tanuki's house. He pushed the door open without taking his house keys out or even touching the latch. It had been unlocked and ajar already, then.

My nostrils flared, letting me scent the air he stirred as he crossed the threshold. Someone else was in there with him, another Tanuki, female, if my nose hadn't been too busted up by Nox earlier. A muffled squeal became a hissing rush of whispers. Beth cocked her head, finally interested in what was going on. Good thing, too. Her hearing always was better than mine.

"Help me up those steps." Beth leaned on the wobbling crutch, and I took her free arm. We went as fast as we could, which meant a regular human pace. In the doorway, the crutch snapped in half. Beth tossed the pieces aside, gripping the door jamb instead.

My sister hopped on one foot through the near pitch-black hallway. I followed along, trailing her by scent through a door at the end. Beth stumbled headfirst into the brightly lit white-tiled kitchen. She caught herself on a long island in the middle, bellying up like it was a bar instead of her dead fiancé's family gathering place.

"Kim!" I stepped around Beth to see who she was greeting. "Why didn't you tell me she'd come back to town, Mr. Ichiro?"

"I didn't know she was here until just a minute ago." Mr. Ichiro's mouth was a thin, straight line. His eyes gleamed, but not with any kind of positive emotion. I felt like we'd walked into a shark tank instead of a homey kitchen.

"Nice to see you again, Beth." Kimiko Ichiro gave her a lopsided grin, then brushed right past my sister. "This is Josh? Why didn't anyone ever introduce us?" She flipped a lock of platinum-tipped brown hair over one shoulder.

Before I could even flinch, her hands slid under my jacket. I stepped back so fast she got caught by surprise. I tapped my foot, glaring down at her hands. Then, I snatched my wallet and phone away from her, stuffing them back in my pockets.

"That's why." I snarled.

"She was just having a little fun, Josh." Beth rolled her eyes. "It's what young Tanuki do. Chill out."

"I'll chill out when she apologizes for lifting an Alpha's wallet."

"Oops." Kim's mouth made a little round 'o' as she gasped. I did not know whether she was kidding. "Had no idea you leveled up. Sorry."

"It won't happen again." Mr. Ichiro locked gazes with his daughter. She looked away first. "Now, Kimi. You'll tell me why you broke into the house instead of calling your old father."

"That's sort of personal." Kimiko looked everywhere except at her father. "You know, the kind of private matter a girl wants to keep between herself and her dad. It's not something a nice girl should discuss in front of a shiny new Alpha."

"Kimiko." He stepped closer to her. "Did you get kicked out of the Academy again?"

"I wouldn't say kicked out, exactly." She shrugged, then

flipped her hair. "It's just that I came to the understanding with the help of a new friend. I had more important things to do than sit in the same classroom every day doing drills just like everyone else." The set of her chin hadn't changed, but the corners of her eyes looked slightly misty. "Also, I can't stand being stuck there while you're here all alone."

"Kimi." Mr. Ichiro sighed, shaking his head. "You're at the Academy because you need the discipline."

"And I can't learn that at the dojo, why?" She glanced at me, then at Beth. "See? This isn't the time or place. We're being the worst hosts in the known universe."

Beth's lean had morphed into a slump. She scratched the patch of hair behind her left ear, a clear tell she was exhausted. The juggernaut of a yawn that burst through her lips made that unquestionable. I shook my head, pissed off at myself all over again at letting her get locked up for days in a place where they hadn't even given her water to wash with.

"Kimiko, help Beth to the back parlor. Then, go upstairs and get her fresh linens and some of your clothes."

"I can't give her a Cherry Blossom gi instead?" Kim couldn't withstand her father's severe glare. "Fine. I have some pajamas she can wear tonight." Her sullen pout morphed into a smile, as shiny and brittle as gilt leaf. "But tomorrow, I'm taking you shopping."

"As long as I can get the apparatus replaced, that sounds awesome." Beth flapped a hand at her stump, then put her arm over Kimiko's shoulders, unfazed by the attempted robbery of her brother and the Tanuki's fickle attitude. All I could do was watch them go, listening to the sound of three legs walking across the hall outside the kitchen.

"I apologize for my daughter's behavior." I turned back to Mr. Ichiro. All the stern tension in his face had melted away, leaving an emptiness I had a hard time looking at.

"It's okay." I shrugged. "She apologized. Girls will be girls."

"She wasn't like this before her brother vanished." He sat at the small table next to a bay window. "But then, you know how that sort of thing can change a person."

"Kind of. I was younger than her when Derek went missing." I took the seat across from him. Somehow, he looked smaller and older than back at the dojo. It made me feel like an even bigger jerk for what I was about to say to him. "Life gets harder. More pressure from the family. No longer a spare, but a full-on heir."

"She was always my heir, young one." His eyes flashed, and he held his head up higher. "Ren was born nearly mundane, just a touch of ability. He took after their mother, you know."

"Interesting how that goes." I leaned my head on my hand. "The boys take after Mom and the girls after Dad."

"You're just repeating words you've heard parents say." His shoulders rolled back out of their slouch. "They'll have new meaning for you someday, with luck. Your mother and father must be in such a state, their son and daughter in this on their own."

"At least we've got each other now." I bowed my head slightly. "And some experienced help."

"I won't be able to do much more than offer Beth a place to stay, I'm afraid." He put his hands flat on the table. "Since I'm representing Miss Phillips once you surrender her to the Sidhe Queen, any assistance I might give you would be a conflict of interest. Yet another thing you have yet to understand fully."

"Surrender Nox? Never. What kind of Alpha would I be if I did something like that?" I tried to swallow my anger but knew its rising was as obvious as the dawn to someone like Mr. Ichiro.

"The just kind." He looked away. "But I suppose you could refuse the Queen, at that. Admit to witnessing Nox's crime, but refuse to make the trade."

"What's the point of that?" I raised an eyebrow. "That'd just make it look like I sided with the Unseelies."

"You mean, you haven't?" It was Mr. Ichiro's turn to raise an eyebrow. "Everybody knows what happened—that she stole a Seelie artifact and undid the Queen's enchantment. Besides, if you surrender Miss Phillips, it might look like you've sided with the Seelies this time. You'll get a reputation for unreliability."

"So this is one of those frying pan and fire situations." I sighed.

"It doesn't have to be. It's not the fact of your refusal that matters, but how prettily you do it." The corners of his mouth turned up slightly as though this was the kind of problem he liked contemplating. I wished I could just let him have it. "If your reason for refusing is to further distance yourself from any perception of bias, for example, your reputation will seem more straightforward."

"See, this kind of thing is why my folks were so happy about Beth and Ren getting official." I shook my head, glad to at least have the old Tanuki's advice. "The two of them could have handled this way better than me."

"Perhaps. However, you're the one responsible for handling it now. I believe you and Miss Phillips will figure out what to do together, just as Beth and Ren may have."

"Wait. What makes you think I'll—" I sighed, shaking my head. "Of course. You saw that whole match."

"I did." His grin was wan but unmistakable. "She's been my student since her family realized she'd need discipline in order to carry on their legacy."

"But that can't happen if the Queen just takes it from her."

"It also can't happen if she doesn't find her mate. Kelpies aren't so different from wolves or Tanuki. We all need companionship, and at least one from each generation must settle down to continue the family line."

"And Nox's brother's an earth magus, so he can't." I shook my head, marveling at how magic could have made a mistake like that. But then again, maybe it hadn't. Coincidence was weirder than those three witchy sisters who harassed Macbeth.

"Yes. Nox's responsibility is double, like Kimiko's. Don't make it harder for both of you by denying even the most unconventional of possibilities."

"But inappropriate relationships are, um, inappropriate." I winced inwardly, hoping it didn't show on my face. "And for wolf shifters, forbidden."

"Perhaps they're not impossible. Coincidence may still have a role to play in all this, but you'll never discover its influence if you avoid the issue." Mr. Ichiro stood. "And now, I must ask you to leave. Please don't stop by again. If you'd like to visit with Beth, send word, and we'll help her meet you elsewhere."

"Thanks, Mr. Ichiro." The last thing I wanted was to leave Beth alone with an old man and a pick-pocketing delinquent, but since my parents had given their blessing when Ren asked for it, I had to be content trusting his family with her safety.

I headed out of the gray house on Angell Street and turned on my heel to make my way toward Swan Point. At least Nox wasn't the only one with explaining to do.

CHAPTER EIGHT

Nox

The air was cold as I set my left fore-hoof on the bank of the Seekonk River. I tossed my head, flinging water off the long slope of my face and through the air behind me. There was a battered-looking boat in the water, but it was almost on the opposite shore in Pawtucket. Glancing around told me I was alone except for a rabbit and a Gnome. The little bunny took off like it was turbo-charged. The Gnome smiled. Their teeth were all made of metal. They sat on top of a toadstool, holding a pipe and snapping their fingers to light it. I didn't have a thing to worry about from them. Gnomes were the smallest Unseelie creatures, like ants to the Sidhe Queen. She'd sooner squash one than listen to a word they might say.

I trotted through denuded underbrush, a few twigs and burrs brushing against my sides. I loved Water magic, but being able to shift into horse form and run free under the moonlight was even more amazing. This wasn't the night for that as much as I might need it. I'd have to explain myself and then go. Lingering would be too dangerous, especially now that I'd seen another Faerie in the area.

Once at the edge of Memorial Grove, I stopped. Shrinking back down to my bipedal shape was like getting out of a roller-coaster car at the end of the ride. Still, I got no protest from the ancestors in my pelt until I moved to disengage it. Echoes of scolds ranging from decades to centuries old rang through my head like the din of rival church bells. At least they all agreed on something—that I shouldn't be out and about without the extra strength and magic the pelt granted its owner. That was what I was, even though I felt like they owned me instead. Once someone took up a Kelpie pelt, it was theirs until they died or put on a different one. It worked the same way for Selkies, the Seelie seal shifters. I wouldn't want to say that five times fast.

I put the pelt away in its oilcloth pouch, adjusted the blanket's drape, and tucked the pouch in a fold. At least it'd be close at hand if something dangerous showed up. I shuddered, thinking about how PPC's own Professor of Summoning got twisted into attacking students. Blaine said he thought it was the Extramagus. It occurred to me, however, that sometimes people just went bad. They couldn't stand something about their lives and snapped. Could that be Josh's uncle's problem, or was he being influenced, too?

A pale sliver of moon came out from behind the clouds. A keening howl rose from the other side of the enormous rock in the middle of the grove. I didn't step into the light until a twig snapped somewhere in front of me. Nice of Josh to do that instead of sneaking up like he could have. When he walked around the other side of the Megalith, my breath caught in my throat. Barely there moonlight made his hair look almost silver instead of blond. His eyes glittered with the fading gold of his recent shift out of wolf form. He tugged at the hem of his shirt, which told me he'd just put it on. I wasn't much surprised to catch a glimpse of firm, defined muscle after sparring with him at the dojo. All the same, it was a nice finish to what had already been a gorgeous view.

"Nice, um—" Josh's eyes moved up, down, and all around. "I've never seen someone wear anything like that before. Is it a dress?"

"Nope," I grinned. My face felt like I'd been standing next to a fire instead of in a wintry breeze. "Blanket."

"There's no way anyone but you could make a blanket look that good." His teeth flashed white in the darkness. Had I been staring at his mouth?

"Thought you'd make some kind of horse joke or something." I barely managed a shrug.

"There's absolutely nothing going on here that's got me in a joking mood." He took a step closer.

"Oh." I found myself unable to move. Well, that's a lie. I trembled a little. Lame, I know, but that's what happens when you stand outside without your Water magic in the middle of February wearing a blanket and no shoes.

"So, you said you have some explaining to do." He tilted his head, peering down at me.

"I know. It's just not the easiest thing to say." It also wasn't easy standing there with this incredibly gorgeous man who pushed me away with one hand and dropped compliments like breadcrumbs from the other. "Listen, I don't like talking around things. I'm going to take a deep breath and just dive into this. This is the kind of stuff I can't unsay and you can't unhear. You still game?"

"Perfectly." He gazed into my eyes. I almost blinked when he used the same word I'd said back at the dojo before agreeing to this meeting. A dig, or coincidence?

"Look, I think you're my mate." I took a breath, ready to just voice all my reasons without thinking about them.

"Been thinking the same. There's one way to see if we're right." Josh put an end to any more talk on the subject.

He pressed closer against me than he'd done during the match, nearly knocking the wind out of me. Then, he touched his lips to mine. I put my arms under his, crossing them under his shirt and over his back. He turned, putting me between himself and the Megalith. His hands were everywhere at first, then they joined forces to try to untie the knot holding my blanket-dress together. He broke our kiss off, leaving me gasping for air. Just as his mouth lowered toward the spot on my neck he'd had me by during our second match, he froze and put one hand to my lips.

"Someone's here." He turned, looking over his shoulder. "Do you smell seaweed?"

I shook my head, not daring to speak. Seaweed this far inland might mean a Selkie, but it could just be a breeze off the harbor. I thought of the Gnome on the toadstool. Could they have been followed, or had a magical device to report that they'd seen me? But that Gnome with the metal teeth wouldn't sell me out. Not when I'd taken their advice about the Sprite business.

"Stay here." Josh whipped off his shirt, then his pants. I tried not to look, but couldn't help it. Fear and desire clashed in my body like fire and ice. I watched him shift, his limbs growing rangier as his run morphed into a lope toward the tree-line. He sniffed the ground, the air, and set off through the trees at full speed.

I heard a howl and a bark, punctuated by a heavy splash and a tiny squeal. Spindly limbs of shrubs in the underbrush shook as Josh returned, something small held in his mouth by the scruff. I recognized it immediately. Even better, I finally remembered where I'd heard of a Gnome with metal teeth before.

"Put them down." I pointed at the little creature. "Maddie and Henry know this Gnome." I did, too, but I wasn't about to tell Josh about that.

Josh dropped them in a heap at my feet, then sat back on his haunches, grinning. His gray fur looked like it was tipped with silver in the low light. I waited for the Gnome to compose themselves, then hunkered down to talk to them.

"Gee Nome." I raised an eyebrow. "Nice to see you, but it's awfully late for you to be out of Henry's apartment."

"I'm here to repay an old favor." They crossed their arms over their chest.

"Okay, well, you're sort of interrupting something important here." I felt my blush reach the roots of my hair.

"It was your wolf who interrupted me." Gee Nome tapped one tiny foot. "You're not the only people who meet here, you know."

"Somehow I doubt you're out on a date." I thought about tapping my own foot in an attempt to look authoritative. Given the blanket dress and the raging blush, I decided not to bother.

"All the same, he interrupted me." The Gnome's voice transitioned from indignation to a squeaky whine. "Can't repay when a wolf chases my debtor away."

"Well, we smelled something like seaweed, and you know how dangerous everything Seelie can be to our kind." I side-eyed the Gnome. They couldn't be too stupid to know that, but they might be drunk. They were lightweights when it came to alcohol.

"Not everything Seelie is Seelie all the time." Gee shifted their weight from one foot to the other, looking like one of those balls that bounce over the words on a karaoke screen. The seaweed smell had to be a Selkie. The Gnome couldn't be talking about anything else.

"That's fine and well, but still it's dangerous." I sighed. "I'll have to get back to campus as fast as I can. It's the only place that's safe."

I felt the displacement of air and rustle of clothing that meant Josh had shifted back. I glanced up at him, disappointed I'd missed the view despite the predicament I was in. I shook my head at the gnome.

"Sorry." Gee raised their hand. I knew they were about to vanish before I could claim a favor.

"Wait. You owe me now, Gee." I pointed at Josh. "Him, too. We're in the biggest bind of our lives, and you interrupted us before we could figure out how to fix it."

"Public place. Not my fault. Already apologized." Gee brought their fingers together.

"No way. She says you owe, you pay." Josh picked Gee up by their hand. "You Vanish us all out of here right away, over to the laundry room in the dorm basement. Then you won't owe me anymore, at least."

"Fine. But only because you're the Gentleman's friend." The moment Josh let go, Gee snapped their fingers.

I hated getting Vanished. It feels like turning to sand and being dumped out by a kid with a broken beach pail. I wondered why Josh was okay with going to campus all of a sudden. Maybe he thought the cemetery was more dangerous than the risk of running into Campus Police. I shook my head, running one hand through my hair as I collected myself. At least it wasn't something I had to do literally.

"And what do I owe the Kelpie?" Gee was fine after vanishing, naturally.

"Tell me who you were meeting with and why." Now I did tap my foot. The coziness of the laundry room had more to do with that than confidence.

"Can't. Prior agreement. You understand." The Gnome smiled. They had me there. They couldn't breach an old contract to fulfill a new one.

"Okay, then." I sighed. "I need a way to get a light sentence in this trial the Queen's got planned."

"Can't do better than a Tanuki lawyer." Gee grinned up at me. Smug little creature probably thought I'd just let them go without paying me if they refused enough times.

"Tell me how Blaine ended up with that sea float." That bit

had been bothering me, since a Seelie artifact shouldn't have ended up with a dragon shifter like that, even with Luck magic on it.

"Prior agreement again. I can only tell you half of that story." Gee shook their head.

"I'll settle for that now and the rest when your agreement expires." I gave them one curt nod. It was good enough.

"Okay!" Gee Nome jumped up, giving themselves a high five behind their back. "I Vanished back in time to make sure the whelp got what you'd need to fight that Spite."

"Wait, what?" Josh blinked. He seemed more disoriented from the Vanishing than me but directed his question properly away from the Gnome. "Gnomes can time-travel?"

"Only a little, and it's weird. There's a whole debate about the fourth dimension." I shrugged, then adjusted my now-slipping blanket.

"It's wibbly-wobbly and timey-wimey, isn't it?" Josh gave me a half-grin.

"Oh, yeah. Especially since Gnomes don't use blue boxes and sonic screwdrivers." I snorted a laugh. "Anyway, I bet that's all Gee has to tell us." I looked down at the Gnome.

"Just one more thing you need to know." They gave me their full metallic smile. "You undoing that enchantment was Lucky. Trust it."

"I'd have to trust you first." I rolled my eyes. Gnomes were about as reliable as other pure Faeries, which meant you only trusted them when you had them under a deal. That last bit felt like an add-on, they might be trying to screw us over with. Then again, they were friends with Henry.

"Up to you." Gee shrugged one little shoulder. "That's it. I'll find you at the end of my prior agreement for the rest." They snapped their fingers and vanished with a faint pop.

"So, do we believe them or not?" Josh rubbed his temples.

"I say we do." I nodded.

"Why?" He shook his head, then blinked a few times.

"Because the sea float's a thing Selkies use. And who was Gee meeting tonight?"

"Once I got to the water, I knew for sure it was a Selkie." Josh frowned. "There were tracks and everything, but they got away before I actually saw them."

"Right. So, I bet that's Gee's prior agreement. Has something to do with that float and a Selkie." I ran a hand through my hair.

"But aren't the Seelies and the Unseelies enemies?" He scratched his head.

"Between pure Unseelies and Selkies, not so much. The King's rules are like a sapling; they bend in the breeze. And Selkies only have a duty to protect the oceans. The Queen counts them as part of her power base, but they're not as bound by her rules as other Seelies, especially when they take their pelts off."

"Makes some sense." He stepped closer to me. "We have, um, a conversation to finish."

"Yes." I stood still, aching for him to touch me again, but not sure whether I could handle it.

"Ahem." Jeannie, the bear shifter Resident Assistant, stood in the laundry room doorway, a basket of disheveled laundry tucked against one hip. "Okay, folks. You don't have to go home, but you can't stay here. Go back upstairs and hang out with whoever you're visiting."

"Okay." Josh took my hand. "Come on, Nox. Let's go find our friends."

I followed him out of the laundry room toward the basement stairs, wondering where he was really taking me.

CHAPTER NINE

Josh

I led her by the hand up the stairs to the first floor, then down the hall to the elevator. After that, I pressed the up button without saying anything, clenching my jaw shut. I wasn't sure I could have a verbal conversation with Nox on the subject of mates. I hadn't had this kind of reaction from my wolf since I was thirteen and dreaming about girls every night. It wanted what it wanted, and I'd have to get my brain around that without Nox around or our interaction on the subject would be purely physical. The way she'd stiffened up told me that might not be the best way to settle this after all. It was like part of her wasn't there or something.

I turned my head, glancing over at her. She stared at the stainless steel elevator doors as they parted, her neck and shoulders held with stiff tension as we stepped into the lift in tandem. She needed to talk to someone before acting on this. Fortunately, I knew just who to leave her with. So did she. We reached for the button marked 5 at the same time.

"You thought of Lynn and Maddie, too?" Her voice was low and soft, like water under a deck on a summer day.

"Yeah." I shrugged with one shoulder. "We told Jeannie we'd go back to our hosts."

The elevator dinged, then opened on an empty hall. I didn't know which room the girls lived in, but I could track humans with no problem. Since Lynn was the only one of those in the dorms, picking up her scent was easy. Almost all the way down the rows of doors, we stopped in front of 566. A gloomy-sounding voice crooned over some intense drum and bass beats, which was definitely Maddie music. Nox knocked.

Lynn Frampton opened the door, her fingertips smeared with about seven different colors of highlighter. Her grin turned into a smile, and her raised eyebrow reminded me of Dr. McCoy from Star Trek. She gave Nox a once-over, then ushered her into the room. I stuck my foot in the door before she could close it on me.

"What gives, Frampton?" I put one hand on the door frame. "Let me in."

"Not by the hair on my chinny chin chin." Lynn threw back her head and guffawed. Nox's throaty laugh and Maddie's barely there titter mingled with it. "This clubhouse is girls only right now, big bad wolf. Go find Bobby. He should be down in his room, editing a Shifter Regulations paper."

"Should have known Darth Lynn would tell me to get lost." I pulled my foot back across the threshold. "Later, ladies."

I headed back down the hall, opting for the stairs this time. Lynn might be a regular human, but she had nearly uncanny instincts when it came to gaging shifter behavior. I needed to blow off some steam, or someone might get hurt. I took the first two flights like a normal person, but the third two steps at a time. On the last, I lifted my feet and slid on my hands down the railings. It took nearly all my willpower to keep my wolf from just turning around, breaking into Lynn's room, and kicking her and Maddie out of there to be alone with Nox.

This time, I tracked a dragon. I stopped by the lounge and peeked in. Blaine was in there without Bobby. He had what looked like an overhead projector with sheets of some kind of parchment scattered all around it. I headed down the hall, checking names on tiny stickers next to the doors instead of using my nose. Too many bears on the first floor. I knocked, and when Bobby answered, he pulled the door all the way open. He waved vaguely at the chair in front of his desk, then picked up his phone to let his thumbs do the texting shuffle.

I turned the chair around and sat in it, pushing the door shut with my toe. I didn't want Blaine walking in on this conversation, especially since I suspected my wolf's ferocity might have something to do with potential competition from a dragon shifter for my mate. Bobby put down the phone and looked up at me.

"Henry's on his way over here. I can already tell your wolf's up. I've never seen your eyes go this gold before. Lynn just pinged to tell me you showed up with Nox wearing a blanket. What's going on?"

"She thinks she's my mate." I leaned my arms on the back of the chair. "My wolf is in extreme agreement with that idea."

"That's awesome!" Bobby's eyes lit up the way they always did when something reminded him of Lynn.

"Nope." I watched him blink and shake his head. Then, I explained about how wolf shifters have to stay neutral when it came to the Faerie Courts. Someone knocked politely on the door.

"Wow." Bobby got up, opening the door. Henry just stood there grinning with his hands in his pockets.

"Dude, you have to invite him in." I rolled my eyes.

"Oh. Sorry, Henry. Come on in." Bobby blushed a little, the boy scout. Half the time, he reminded me of Steve Rodgers in the Captain America comics.

"Thanks." My Beta, the vampire, closed the door most of the way, walked in, and sat on the edge of Blaine's bed.

"Sitting in a dragon's nest." I shook my head. "Aren't you a little flammable for that?"

"We have an understanding." Henry smirked. "I'm too useful for him to fry me. Memory Psychics generally are to history buffs. So Bobby says you're having wolf problems?"

"Yeah, well." I shrugged. My shoulders were getting a workout lately in that regard. "It's Nox."

"You know, I kind of figured." Henry grinned with his lips closed. He still worried about freaking us out with his fangs. "What is she, your mate or something?"

"Were you listening in?" My eyes felt like pinballs, the way they kept rolling.

"No way. You have any idea how annoying amping up my hearing is in a dorm? All the stereos and televisions." He wrinkled his nose. "It'd be like trying to hear a needle in a haystack. Look, it was just kind of obvious over intersession. Anyway, is she or not?"

"Still not sure. My wolf thinks so. But it's a problem." I repeated all the stuff I'd told Bobby and then added in what had happened over at the Megalith in Swan Point. "Once she said that it was like my wolf practically took over."

"Woah." Bobby blinked. "Well, that's what happened to my bear with Lynn. Except sleepier. Because of all the snow and that pesky hibernation stuff."

"Looks like Josh has more standing between him and Nox than you guys had, though." Henry rubbed his chin.

"What do you mean?" Bobby leaned forward, glancing from me to Henry. "You guys know the Extramagus was trying to kill Lynn, right?"

"No. I did not know that." I ran a hand through my hair. "Is that why you and Blaine were on about that theory even before the Summoner problem?"

"Yeah." Bobby's eyebrows crinkled. "Hey, do you think the Extramagus might have something to do with this whole thing too?"

"No idea." I tapped my chin with one finger. "The thing is, pack issues happen all the time. And what Nox did, well the Queen's reaction isn't out of the ordinary according to her or Fred." I looked at Henry, who seemed lost in thought. "What do you think, Henry?"

"I was at the bank this morning, you know." He blinked, then looked from Bobby to me. "Found an amulet with a memory about a Selkie pelt gone missing a few years back, right after PPC changed its admissions policy. The Queen accused a Troll family of stealing it, but nothing came from that. We should look that case up. It might just be a legal precedent, but it could have coincidental implications."

"Wait, a Troll family? I remember reading something about that case for Advanced Ecology." Bobby pulled open his laptop. I saw him navigate to the PLEXIS Nexus. "This is probably something we want Olivia to look at sometime. She's the Extrahuman Law major."

"Well, what've you got for now?" I tried to look at his laptop, but couldn't without getting up. I stayed put.

"Looks like these Trolls protect the Mount Hope Bridge, between Portsmouth and Warren. The Tollands, all Unseelie, it looks like. A thorough search of all their assets didn't turn up the pelt." Bobby scrolled down, skimming the text on the screen. Lynn's study habits must have rubbed off on him. "A Selkie died in an accident there, and his pelt went missing."

"Wait, a minute. What was the date of that accident?" I felt like the pit of my stomach had turned to ice.

"March 15, four years ago." Bobby glanced up, then leaned back when he looked at my face.

"My sister Beth lost her leg on that bridge the same night." I swallowed hard past the lump in my throat. "Her fiancé died, too. Ren Ichiro."

"Huh. Ichiro's the name of the attorney on this report. Yoshi Ichiro."

"That's Ren's dad." I shook my head. "Beth is staying with him."

"Sounds more and more like we should consider this coincidence." Bobby looked up, his eyes wide and his nostrils flared. "The Extramagus tried to use an old accident to attack Lynn and old hate crimes to hurt Henry. We'd better run this by Blaine."

"Nothing doing." I shook my head, crossing my arms over my chest. "It's none of his business."

"Josh. You've got to get over this whole rivalry with the dragon thing." Henry sighed. "He just flirts with everyone. I mean, you should have seen what happened every time he remembered Maddie for a while."

"I want to let it go, man. But my wolf can't get over it unless the mate thing's resolved." I shook my head. "And that's just not a good idea."

"But you also can't just avoid Nox and Blaine." Henry leaned forward, staring me down. The alliance medallion under my shirt grew cold against my skin. "They're part of your pack, remember? Plus Blaine's the one with all the Extramagus information, and we need to know whether his hand is in this."

"The fact he's my pack-mate makes it worse. I can't be around him right now without a conflict we can't afford." I clenched my fists on the sides of the chair back. "This Extramagus is a major douche. Almost as bad as Blaine himself."

Bobby's mouth dropped open at the same time Henry's did. Their expressions would have been mirror images if Henry hadn't had fangs. The vampire's hand moved slowly up to hide them from view. Hurried heavy footsteps headed away from the door down the hall. I leaped up, pushing through and leaning out to see Blaine turn the corner into the lounge, his head and shoulders down. When I turned to step back into the room, I almost bumped into Jeannie.

"Wow, Josh." The blonde bear shifter shook her head, reminding me of Beth's big sister act from before the accident. "You should go apologize."

"Maybe he should apologize for listening in." I put my hands on my hips like I would have if I'd been talking to Beth. "Smart guy like him should know better."

"This is his room you're talking about him in, you know." Jeannie tried to look down her nose at me, impossible since she was more than a head shorter. Her disdain shouldn't have shaken me, but it did.

"And I'm his Alpha," I growled.

"So act like it." She tilted her chin up, snarling. Was this really the same girl Lynn said reminded her of a Barbie doll? "You lay things on the line with him. It's one thing people say they admire about your mom, Dennison. Fill her shoes."

"Who do you think you are, telling me how to head my own pack?" I loomed over her.

"I'm the Resident Assistant tasked with keeping these kinds of problems from trashing the campus. Now get down to that lounge and have it out. Take it outside to the park if you've got to get physical. And you're welcome." Jeannie spun on her heel and stalked down the hall, reminding me for all the world of Fleur Delacour telling Mrs. Weasley off in the Harry Potter books.

"Well, that settles it, then." Henry brushed past me into the hall. "You want me to tell Blaine to meet you down at India Point?"

"No." I took a deep breath, leashing my wolf with the cold feeling that still hadn't left the pit of my stomach. "But you guys should come with me, anyway."

"Sure thing." Bobby shut his laptop and set it down on the desk.

We headed down the hall, me in front with Henry and Bobby

flanking me on the right and left. The whole walk could have been filmed in slow-mo and put into a movie montage. I focused on what I'd have to say, the questions I'd need to answer to bury the mate competition hatchet with Blaine so we could move past the bullshit. Henry had been right. It was the reason I'd made him my Beta. I couldn't sideline Blaine for this. Even if the pack problems had nothing to do with that Extramagus, I'd still need them all by my side when we went to get my folks back. The way that letter was addressed meant I had to do things officially, and that meant bringing everyone in my pack, including the dragon shifter, as infuriatingly arrogant as he was most of the time.

"Blaine. We're talking now." I strode across the room, leaning on the patch of wall between two windows. "Shut the door, Henry." My Beta followed the order. Bobby sat on the arm of the sofa Blaine had sprawled out on.

"Oh, okay. Because what I really need on top of all my own stress is an interview with the Alphahole." Blaine's eyes narrowed, a red spark rising in them. They were also slightly bloodshot and shiny at the corners. I flared my nostrils, scenting a hint of salt and brimstone as he puffed out a smoke ring. Hadn't Lynn mentioned something about Blaine being as lonely as she felt sometimes?

"Yeah, I've been a douchecanoe." I held my hands out, palms up. "But it's temporary. Part of the reason I'm here is to offer you an apology. But before you go thanking me and accepting it, we have to talk about my mate."

"What to the who now?" Blaine sat up, tapping his ear. "I thought I heard you say the word mate, but you don't have one of those."

"It's a recent development and nothing's final yet." I took a deep breath, summoning all my calm and applying it to keeping my wolf down. "But you'd better leave Nox Phillips alone if you want to keep things copacetic."

"Wait," Blaine smirked. Then he snorted. He put one hand

over his mouth, snickering behind it. Bobby tilted his head, glaring at his roommate as though a bear stare could get a dragon to shut up.

My wolf practically caught fire, leaping up within me, daring me to shift and go for Blaine's throat. I clenched my jaw and fists, fighting to keep control. Even with all that effort, I could feel my eyes going gold, the hair on my arms and the back of my neck raising as a low growl clawed its way out of my throat.

"I think you need to explain things better than that, Blaine." Henry's words, delivered in a cool deadpan, helped me focus.

"No, I mean seriously." Blaine took a deep breath and let it out with a little trickle of smoke. "Hold on a minute. Nox? Do you have any idea why I even flirted with her in the first place?"

I shook my head, knowing that if I tried to speak my wolf might just bust out and attack.

"I was trying to get Maddie and Henry together." Blaine shook his head. "I mean, she's smoking hot in the looks department, but way too intense. Not my type at all. If she's your mate, go for it. You guys'd be awesome together."

Bobby punched Blaine in the shoulder. That one brotherly gesture instantly settled my wolf, reminding me of Derek's face as he went with the Shifter Registry Feds, leaving me hidden in the brush next to the rain shelter on the Blackstone Boulevard bike path. I never told Beth or my parents that his disappearance had been my fault. He'd taken the rap for me during my first change, which happened in public before it was legal. Somehow, the FBE had known exactly where to look for us. I hadn't thought about how weird that was since the night it happened.

"Where did you go, Beowulf?" At first, I didn't realize it was Blaine who'd spoken. I'd never heard him talk without a zing of sarcasm or the disdained Long Island lockjaw.

"Just thinking about how far back all this mess might go. I'm going to need your help." I dropped my hands to my sides, finally able to relax my shoulders. "So. I'm sorry for acting like an Alphahole when I should just be an Alpha."

"Apology accepted." Blaine smiled, like an actual smile instead of a jerk-smirk. Then, the Long Island lockjaw returned like Aragorn to Gondor. "Now what's all this about needing my help?"

CHAPTER TEN

Nox

Lynn's joke about the big bad wolf hadn't been that funny, but her laughter was downright infectious. Even Maddie came down with a bad case of the giggles. I wasn't left as breathless by laughter as I'd been by Josh's affections earlier, but it was a near thing. The tears at the corners of my eyes couldn't decide whether they were stress relief or anguish or the awkwardness of my mating predicament.

"Okey-doke." Lynn sat at her desk then ran one hand through her hair, pulling it back over her shoulder like a curtain. "Now that the fun's over, I have to ask you a personal question, Nox. Why were you out in the middle of the night with Josh Dennison in nothing but your undies and a military surplus blanket?"

"Well, I could tell you a long story or a short one." I took a deep breath, trying a relaxation technique to keep from blushing. "Which version do you want?"

"Oooh, both!" Maddie clapped her hands together. "Give us the short one first, though."

"Don't you have any respect for spoilers, sweetie?" Lynn rolled her eyes.

"Nope. Can't stand the suspense." Maddie tossed her head, curls cascading over the right side of her face. "Sit down and dish."

"Okay." I sat gingerly on the edge of Maddie's bed next to where she'd patted it, then crossed my ankles. "Well, I met Josh out at Swan Point. Told him I think he's my mate."

"Oh. My. God!" Lynn sprung up from her seat. "No way! So you are? I mean, he is? I mean. I can't even believe this right now; this is so crazy!"

"Um." I blinked, completely puzzled by Lynn's weird behavior. She never got like this over anything but an A+ grade. "Well, we're still not sure."

"Oh, boy. Well, I've been there. I can't believe it. So, Swan Point. Isn't it a bit, um, cold out there for, um—"

"Lynn, chill on all the gritty detail questions." I'd almost forgotten Maddie was there until she spoke up and put her hand on my arm. "She's not wearing her pelt. What went wrong, Nox?"

"Besides the fact that any relationship between Josh and me is kind of forbidden because wolf shifters keep it neutral with the Faerie Courts?" I sighed and blinked. Had I been this close to tears all the way over here?

"Oh, no. I forgot." Lynn put her head in her hands. "Me and my big mouth. I'm sorry."

"It's okay," I lied. Lynn meant well; her wit just worked faster than her heart sometimes. It wasn't her, but the situation that had me down.

"No, it's absolutely not okay." Lynn shook her head. "Hey, you don't have a bag or anything." She got up, making a beeline for her dresser. "You can't go home in a blanket on a night like this."

Lynn rummaged around until she found a PPC sweatshirt. "This is too long on me, so it'll probably work for you."

Lynn was shorter than me and curvy. I took the shirt and held it against my chest. It'd fit me across the shoulders just fine. She kept looking through the drawers, but all her pants would have had trouble staying up on my lack of hips.

"I'll get her something for the bottom." Maddie went straight to the lowest drawer of her dresser, unrolling a pair of gray yoga pants that looked way too long for her. "They sent me a tall instead of a short, and I washed them before I figured it out."

"Thanks, guys." I pulled the pants on under the blanket and then the sweatshirt over my head. Before putting my arms through the sleeves, I undid the knot holding the makeshift dress together. The wool was stubborn, practically glued together after being in brackish water and mauled by a randy wolf shifter. My face heated as I flushed with the memory of Josh's urgency. I hadn't known what to do at the time and probably wouldn't if it happened again.

"Wow." Lynn shook her head. "That looks like how I feel when I think about Bobby." I looked up to see her pointing at my reddening face. "Is it really so impossible for the two of you to be together?"

"I don't know." I put my arms in the sleeves, then pulled the blanket out from under the sweatshirt. "I've never heard of a wolf shifter finding a Faerie mate, or even an untithed Changeling."

"But he has a sister, though." Maddie chewed her bottom lip. "And she's older than him. Can't she take the packs over instead of him? I mean, a mate is a huge big deal with wolf shifters. They go nuts if they don't find one by middle age."

"Her mate died, and she still hasn't found another. A single wolf shifter can't run an established pack. It's even worse that I'm unsuitable." I shook my head. "It's like coincidence saying Josh's Uncle Jake is the right leader after all."

"Wait a minute." Maddie tapped her temple with one finger.

"Hold on and let me look something up." She reached over and pulled a textbook about coincidence off her desk. I'd forgotten she was taking a course on that already. Something like a growl sounded in the small room. It took me a few seconds to realize it went along with the empty feeling in my gut.

"While we wait, you need some food." Lynn opened the drawer on her nightstand and chucked a few Power Bars at me. "They taste like cardboard according to Bobby, but they do the trick when he's hungry after shifting." She watched me tear up the wrappers and chew on one of the bars. "Wait. How did you shift without your pelt?"

"I didn't." My words came out all muffled and garbled around the gluey wannabe food, but Lynn seemed to understand them, anyway. A side-effect of being a bear shifter's mate, probably. I pulled the oilskin pouch from a fold in the blanket while swallowing. "That's all part of the long story Maddie wanted me to skip." I gave them the full account of my trip down the tunnel and swim up the river while Maddie looked things up.

Lynn opened her mouth, about to ask a question judging by the look on her face. Three firm raps on the door interrupted her. She got up and opened the door just as Maddie scrawled notes down on a piece of loose-leaf paper. Jeannie stood in the doorway for just a moment before shouldering past Lynn without so much as an invitation.

"You ladies should take this whole show down to the first-floor lounge. Everyone's there except Tony and Olivia." Jeannie stood next to Lynn's desk with her hands on her hips. Maddie collecting her notes and the RA's tapping foot were the only sounds for a moment. Lynn grabbed her backpack and headed out, Maddie following close behind. Jeannie let me out but stopped me with a hand on my shoulder as she shut the door to 566 behind her. I turned and stared.

"What is it?" I lowered my eyebrows. The last thing I needed was a lecture from a bear shifter who looked like she belonged on a CW show.

"Settle down." Her eyes were wide with an empathy that stopped my anger in its tracks. "I only just realized you don't have a place to stay. Can't go back to your off-campus apartment, huh?"

"Yeah, you're right." I turned my head, eying her warily. "I've had a little help, though."

"Not enough, from the looks of it." Jeannie tilted her head to the side, looking more like a cocker spaniel shifter than a were-bear. "You need a hot shower. A bathroom with a real mirror. An actual bed."

"So? I got myself in trouble." I shrugged, holding my hands palms up to either side. "What's your point?"

"I can put you up for the weekend," she said. "The RA up on three has to go home for a wedding tomorrow. I'll stay in her room, and you can have mine while she's gone."

"Wow, Jeannie." I blinked my suddenly stinging eyes. "Thank you. I really owe you one."

"No, you don't." She smiled.

"I don't understand." I ran a hand through my hair, suddenly almost too weary to stand.

"It's the least I can do. What you did for that Spite might have pissed off the Queen, but it was the right thing to do in my book." Jeannie reached out and patted my shoulder. "Besides, I work for Student Life. You're a student with a life, so why shouldn't I help you? Now, get down to the first-floor lounge and talk to your friends. I'll ask Olivia to bring you over after your class tomorrow, tell her you're room-sitting."

I nodded, stifling a yawn, then shuffled down the hall. I was too tired to do much besides lean against the elevator wall on the way down. After the chime went off a second time, I blinked, just barely getting my hand between the doors so I could stop them from closing. I stepped out of the elevator on the first floor, heading for the sounds of my friends' voices and almost ran headlong into Tony Gitano. I hadn't spoken to him since our odd conversation in the Nocturnal Lounge the night Josh fled his home.

"So, they're finally thinking the Extramagus has something to do with all this." Tony smirked.

"Are they?" I could have slapped him for not telling them sooner.

"Yup. Jeannie called me over here." He took a step back from me, covering for his fear by leaning against the wall.

"She's well informed, isn't she?" I turned, taking two steps toward the lounge. If he wanted to continue being hinky, he'd have to do it on the way down the hall.

"Less than I am." Hurried footsteps punctuated his words. "Her connections are mostly from out-of-town."

"You really are pretty shady." I tried to ignore the chilly tile against my bare feet as I listened to his squeaky sneakers.

"You're entitled to that opinion." Tony caught up, coming into view in my peripheral vision.

"It's going to catch up to you someday." I shook my head.

"I've still got some of my nine lives left." He chuckled, but his eyes stayed flat and weary.

"That's not a myth?" I rubbed my eyes in tandem with another tummy rumble.

"You're entitled to your opinion of my multiple lives. And some food. Bobby ordered pizza. Go on in, but not a word about our previous conversation." Tony poked me in the bicep with one index finger.

"Why should I keep my mouth shut about that? It's useful information." I was too tired and hungry to deal with Tony's dodgy hangups.

"Then don't credit the source." Tony glared up at me. "You almost drowned me like a three-legged kitten last week. You owe me."

"Fine." I mimed zipping my lips. "No credit for Tony G. For now."

"Appreciate it." The little jerk held the door for me.

I stepped in, walking past everyone else and heading straight for the unoccupied sofa in the corner. The cushions felt like heaven, but my empty stomach kept me from falling asleep. The mingled conversation was hard to follow, but I didn't mind. Everyone was busy catching each other up, Lynn filling the less sordid details of my story into Josh's account. Henry headed over, sitting on the other end of the couch.

"You okay?" The vampire's brow furrowed.

"Nothing some food and a nap won't fix. Thanks for asking." I blinked, hoping I didn't look sleepier than Olivia.

"Least I can do for someone who helped save my life." He set his elbows on his knees, then folded his hands to rest his chin on them "Speaking of which, you have Seelie problems. It might be time to call in one of those favors from the Sprite. What do you think?"

"Probably. I'll need a safe place to do that." I sat up. "Oh! I can make one."

"What do you mean you can make one?" I hadn't noticed Blaine was there until after he spoke.

"Mr. Waban gave me some church-keys." I yawned.

"Tiamat's Scales!" He sat. Well, not really. More like his knees buckled when he happened to be standing in front of a chair. "I haven't heard of the old serpent even selling one since the nineteenth century."

"Serpent?" I raised an eyebrow. "What do you mean?"

"You didn't know?" Blaine snorted out a couple of smoke rings. "Taki Waban's a tough old drake of the ice variety. He was here before Mother came to the continent. No one even knows how old he is."

"Wow." No wonder Blaine had been afraid of him. Dragon shifters only got more powerful with age. It was one reason Mrs.

Harcourt was adored from afar and with no small measure of fear. Her husband was centuries younger than her. I wondered what the story was there.

"Mother will be so jealous if she finds out you got your hands on those." He leaned in like a conspirator. "She'll never let you hear the end of it. Literally. She's always wanted some church-keys for her hoard. It's one of the few magic items she's missing, and Mr. Waban refuses to sell them to her at any price she's offered."

"Well, maybe she should try pissing off a Faerie Monarch or two." Josh sat down next to me. "I bet Taki Waban's keys cost bold action, not gold."

"I bet that's true." Blaine gave Josh a huge grin. "What'll you wager?"

"I've gambled enough to last the rest of the year, thanks." Josh stood. "Pizza's here." He strode over and brought back a whole box. That was okay since Bobby had ordered six.

We sat in the lounge, sharing pizza and information for a couple of hours. Tony eyed me briefly when I brought up the Extramagus's family tree, but no one questioned where I'd gotten the idea, anyway. Lynn just made a note to add genealogy to the future research list.

I nodded off on the sofa. When Josh shook my shoulder to wake me, everyone but Henry had gone. Josh left for his house, which he could finally return to. I wanted to go with him, help straighten up the place, but it was too dangerous. Instead, Henry brought me to the Nocturnal Lounge. I curled up with the bedroll from the bottom of my rucksack in the corner behind the vampire's favorite study table, relieved that it might be the last time I'd have to sleep there.

CHAPTER ELEVEN

Josh

I needed help. Unfortunately, I couldn't admit that to anyone in my pack except Henry and the sun was up. I picked up the phone and told Siri I had to talk to Beth. Don't get the idea that I'm an iFanboy; my parents buy the phones, and that's what they like. I'd be switching to Android once I was the one pulling the purse strings.

The phone rang twice as I imagined Adele's "Hello" blaring out of Beth's speakers while my face popped up on the screen. Yeah, that's a freakily depressing song, but what else do you expect a girl with one leg and a dead fiancé to want to listen to? Even Maddie's old goth music was too upbeat for my sister.

"Beth's phone, Kim speaking. Can I direct you to call someone cuter and less of a downer instead?"

My sister's voice took on a strident tone I hadn't heard since the day before the accident. Beth had been nothing but exhausted or weepy in all that time. Maybe the pick-pocketing Tanuki wasn't such a bad influence after all. I held the expensive white rectangle away from my ear as the muffled whoosh soundtrack of their struggle for the phone continued.

"What is it?" Beth's voice just barely drowned out the sound of Kimiko Ichiro's juvenile raspberry.

"Gotta talk. Some new information and ideas came up last night, and I need someone to bounce them off of."

"As long as you don't ask me if I want to build a snowman." Beth actually snorted out an honest to goodness laugh after that. So she'd paid attention the year that Frozen movie came out and I stood outside on the back lawn below her window blasting the damn song out of Derek's old boom-box like I was John freaking Cusak. Good.

"I promise. No snowmen." I snorted back. "Just an interview with your kid brother about a bunch of crazy theories."

"No whiny vampires named Louis, either." I heard a muffled protest about Brad Pitt's hotness and then another raspberry in the background.

"Okay." We'd never get off the phone with all the side-chatter. "What in Luna's name is Baby Metal doing over there, pretending she's two?"

"Baby Metal?" Beth full out guffawed. "Oh, that is rich!" I heard another tussle for the phone, then a click as it went to speaker.

"Who do you think you are, calling me Baby Metal? You big jerk!"

"You should meet some of his friends." Beth's voice told me she was either waggling her eyebrows or winking. Kimiko let out a frustrated little squeak.

"So, where do we meet?"

"I got it!" Kimiko squealed, her voice closer as she grabbed the phone and took it off speaker. "I'll text the address." Then she hung up.

And that was how I ended up in a Wickenden Street nail

salon. I walked in, blinking at the design choices. Yellow paint with pink trim gave the entire place a girly vibe, and the endless chatter of the staff as they held hands and feet with the all-female clientele provided constant background noise. At least they weren't playing junk pop.

I spotted Kimiko right away. She waved, bouncing up and down in her seat, splashing a little puddle on the floor next to the spa her feet were submerged in. I closed the distance between us, determined to grab her by the shoulders and shake them while giving her a stern lecture about bringing a woman with only one foot for a pedicure. Luckily, I glanced at Beth before doing any such thing.

My sister's smile was even bigger than Kimiko's. She may have had only one foot in the spa instead of the usual two, but the woman helping her didn't act any differently than the one with Kimiko. I couldn't smile, but my embarrassment evaporated the sour look off my face right quick.

"We can talk here?" I raised an eyebrow.

"Sure," Beth grinned. "No one expects wooj in a nail salon."

"Fine, then." I leaned against the wall. "So, our problem doesn't just come from what happened at the end of Intersession. It goes all the way back to the night of your accident. Maybe further than that."

"Wait, really?" Beth's eyebrows threatened to meet her hairline. I had no idea why Kimiko giggled with one hand over her mouth and one pinkie sticking up.

"Excuse me." An unfamiliar female voice came from somewhere near my elbow.

"Uh, sorry. Am I in your way?" The last thing I wanted was to stand in the middle of where the nail-doers had to walk.

"No..." The woman shook her head, placing one ironically unpainted finger on her cheek. "It's just that, um, this area's for paying customers only, sir."

"Here!" Kimiko waved a pair of twenties in the air. "Sit down. My treat!"

I turned, intending to just leave and wait until they walked out of that yellow and pink house of humiliation, but my knees buckled. An unoccupied staff member whisked off my combat boots and socks. Before you could say "annoying Tanuki brat," I had my feet in a whirlpool right next to my sister.

"At least there's no snowmen or vampires named Louis, huh Josh?" Beth's giggly delivery and the sparkle in her eyes was worth the embarrassment.

All I could do was roll my eyes and let out a low growl. Having to deal with Kimiko was nearly as bad as hanging out with Blaine. I'd never met her before, not even through the year Beth had dated Ren. They clearly knew each other pretty well, though.

"Okay, so like I was saying." I cleared my throat, trying not to laugh. The whirlpool tickled a little. "There's a report that the other car in the accident belonged to a Selkie."

"And we should care about that drunk bastard, why?"

"Because his pelt went missing." I blinked as the pink-smocked staff member pulled my foot out of the spa and went to work massaging some kind of lotion on it. "Friends of mine think that's the real problem here, the reason the um," I glanced around. You never knew who might be a Changeling, even in a nail salon.

"Okay, so the Queen's angry because she thinks someone has something of hers?" Beth nodded. "Makes sense. Also tells us why she's focused on Nox in particular. She had to use something Seelie in order to turn that Spite back into a Sprite. Maybe the Queen thinks she has the Selkie pelt."

"Oh yeah." Kimiko twirled her hair. "She'd want that back for sure. Especially since those Monarchs can't make any more pelts unless they get back together."

"Well, that's not happening." I crossed my arms over my

chest. The massage felt pretty decent, but I was afraid I'd end up with neon toenails or something, so it was hard to relax. "Anyway, I was there. She used a glass sea float, not a Selkie pelt."

"Good thing, too." Kimiko nodded. I didn't like her grin. "Do you have any idea how much those pelts go for if you can find a buyer who won't talk?"

"Leaping Luna!" I glared at the Tanuki. "No wonder your dad sent you to the Academy." That place was like Extrahuman Community College on lockdown.

"Woah, kid bro." Beth patted my hand. "Chill. She happens to know something about magic items. Maybe you could use her help."

"Info, yes. Direct help, no thanks." I shrugged. "Look, sorry about the school remark, okay. But I already have a magical artifact expert in my pack."

"Oh yeah, the dragon shifter, right?" Beth scratched her head. "What was his name again? Blake?"

"No." I sighed. "Blaine Harcourt. His mom owns three Newport mansions and the biggest hoard in this hemisphere. He grew up around magic items."

"Wow." Kimiko's eyes lit up like a Mall Christmas tree. "You know the Harcourts?"

"Just one of them." Hopefully, she'd leave it at that.

"Do you get invited to their parties or anything?" Her interest seemed shady. Either that or the Harcourts were a bigger deal than I'd thought.

"No." I sighed through a clenched jaw. "Look, we're getting off the subject here."

"Okay, so how do you think this information about the pelt will help?" Beth chewed her bottom lip. "Nox still undid what she undid and everything, so she will get punished, regardless."

"Right, but it might be just a slap on the wrist if we can find that dead Selkie's pelt and turn it over."

"True." Kimiko nodded. "It'd be a fair exchange, one enchantment for another. Seelie law is all about balance."

"So what kind of thing might she ask for if we don't get the pelt, then?"

"Why's that so important to you?" Kimiko looked down her nose at me.

"Because I think Nox and I are mates." I might have answered Kimiko's question, but I directed my answer at Beth.

"I understand." Beth nodded. "You want to protect her as much as you can. If the Queen suspects Nox of hiding a Selkie pelt, she'll want a Kelpie pelt in return."

"I also can't stand the idea of her giving up a part of herself because she saved my Beta's unlife." I told them both the story. Kimiko hadn't been around, and Beth had acted more dead than Henry until today.

"Wow. I didn't know that's why she did it." Kimiko grinned a little, losing the bratty veneer. She looked troubled, maybe even a little sad. "Huh."

"So, what did they do to look for the pelt?" Beth had her phone out, swiping and tapping.

"Just about everything you can think of. They even had Maddie's dad out here scrying." I shook my head. "Human and Extrahuman effort for almost a year, all focused on finding an unattached Selkie pelt."

"Would it have degraded by now, though?" Beth gave me a wan smile. "I feel out of my depth on this. Got no idea how the magic pelts work."

"Well, they're all aligned with water. That's why they're stored in oilcloth. If they dry completely out, they're toast." The facts rolled out of Kimiko's brain like they usually did for Lynn Frampton. She ignored the woman dabbing gold paint on her toenails. "Kelpie pelts need to be in fresh water, and Selkie pelts need salt. That bridge was over salt water, so if it fell in, it'd be okay."

"It was, was it?" Something bothered me about Kimiko's little speech, but I couldn't put my finger on it. "Hey, what if the reason no one's been able to find the damn thing is because someone picked it up and put it on?"

"Huh." Beth chewed on that for a minute. "That'd explain why they couldn't find it. Well one of the possible reasons, anyway."

"What other reason can you think of?" It was my turn to scratch my head. I was stumped. That was the reason I had super-geniuses in my pack, after all.

"Theft!" Kimiko's outburst smacked of nervousness. "Either kind of pelt is super valuable like I said. Dragon hoard valuable, even. Isn't that bridge near Newport?"

"It is. But I don't think Blaine would have…I mean, he's not my favorite person in the world, but he's no thief."

"But what about his parents?" Kimiko twirled her hair again, looking just about everywhere except at my eyes. "They're supposed to be big-time opportunists, especially his step-dad. Did they help in the search?"

"Dunno. Have to look at the records again." I wondered if Kimiko was fishing for information about the Harcourts or deliberately misinforming me. "But value aside, they're awfully hidebound to do something that, well, underhanded. Hoards are full of trophies. If there isn't some kind of conquest or right of possession behind an item, dragons aren't all that interested in it."

"You're right." Beth scratched her head. "What makes more sense is, some regular Joe or Jane picked it up thinking this was their chance to be an Extrahuman."

"But that'd be so illegal they'd never be able to really benefit from it."

"Well, what if he or she had nothing much to lose?" Beth sighed. "A Selkie skin would make it easy to live off the grid. For a person running from something, or who thought they had no other choice, it'd be a pretty easy decision to make."

"Point and match, Beth." If anyone knew desperation, it was

my sister. I looked down to find the nail lady drying my feet with a little towel. My feet looked…decent. They'd spared me the indignity of putting polish on, thank goodness.

I pulled on my socks and laced up my boots. The girls had already waited for their toes to dry. We headed across the street to the cafe where I let Kimiko and Beth gab over quadruple lattes or whatever. Somebody had that pelt. It'd be amazeballs with a side of awesomesauce if I could find them and present them to the Queen before Nox's trial. Of course, I'd also have to get through an Alpha contest against my uncle. No pressure, right?

CHAPTER TWELVE

Nox

Staying awake in my Local Extrahuman History class was easier today than it had been since the Spring semester started. I had Watkins, of course. He was the only Professor who taught that here except Brodsky. Since it was kind of my fault Watkins got stuck teaching two sections of a Junior level course along with the Freshman level Ecology class he constantly complained about, I'd been determined not to give him any headaches.

"If you can't get through one of my lectures without double-fisting coffee, you'll be warming the same seat next semester, Phillips." Half the heads in the room turned in my direction. Lucky break, I guess.

"Sorry, Professor." I stifled a yawn and tucked one of the Styrofoam cafeteria cups under my seat.

"So, as I was saying before some genius down at the dining hall led a horse shifter to coffee, the hurricane barrier went up around the time most of your parents were born. What else went up with it?"

"Ooh! I know!" Only one hand shot up front and center in the room. It was pale, long-fingered, and not quite human.

"Does anyone besides Albert have a clue?" Professor Watkins tapped the toe of one wingtip shoe behind his podium.

"Wards." I yawned. "They went up all along the coast in a great big circle. But they cut off at Tiverton, right in the middle of the Pell Bridge."

"Well, this is a pleasant surprise. It seems Phillips cares more about passing than just about any of you." Watkins' smile reminded me of sharks and crocodiles. "So tell me, Phillips, who put those wards up, anyway?"

Unfortunately, I had no clue. I remembered the wards from Tinfoil Hat's chat the night before, not from the textbook. Sighing, I almost gave up and shook my head until I remembered something Blaine and Henry had mentioned the last week of Intersession. I had a snowball's chance in hell of being right but would take that over zero chance any day of the week.

"Stanhope. He was an Extramagus, right?"

"Are you right?" The smile on Watkins' face didn't budge. "You tell me."

"Yes." I nodded with as much confidence as I could muster. "Stanhope. He was an Extramagus. He's the guy who made the wards."

"And does anybody know why he didn't bother with Tiverton?" Watkins turned away, pacing along the front of the lecture hall in search of his next victim. I sighed into my coffee, relieved I'd been correct.

About halfway between my back-row seat and Albert down in front, a woman nearly as pale as he was stood up. Olivia the amazing diurnal owl shifter. Her birdlike frame was emphasized by the feathery layers of nearly white hair on her head. Leave it to a bookworm bird shifter to be blessed with the ghost of Farrah Fawcett's best hair days.

"Adler. Tell all the people who didn't bother with the assigned reading why Stanhope refused to ward Tiverton."

"Because back then, the biggest community of Unseelies in Rhode Island lived over there, and he was trying to curry favor with the Queen." She shifted her weight from one foot to the other. "Sir."

"And she remembered to call me sir, which is more than the rest of you louts bother with." Watkins clapped slowly. "I'll let all you slackers go as long as you remember this little tidbit that's going on next week's quiz."

He leaned against the podium, lowering his voice so much everyone stopped packing their things away in order to hear him. "Extramagi are some of the most powerful people in the world. But history tells us all that power's still never enough for them. They'll do absolutely anything, even the last thing you'd imagine, in order to get more. Extramagi. Greedy fargin icehole bastiches." He straightened. "Anyone who emails me with the movie that catch-phrase is from and which character said it gets two extra credit points on the quiz. Now get out of here."

I gulped down the rest of the coffee in the cup still on the tiny swivel desk in front of me, then reached down and grabbed the still-full cup under my seat. When I sat up again, Olivia stood blinking down at me. It must have been a novel experience for her since the only person in Tinfoil Hat her height was Maddie, and she loved stompy platform boots. Olivia always seemed to wear Converse high-tops or ballet flats. Today, she had on the latter.

I yawned at exactly the same time she did, the drawn-out breaths turning into a chuckle and a giggle, respectively. I tucked the coffee in the crook of one arm, then slung my rucksack over the other shoulder. Before I could move the desk piece, a shadow fell over it. I looked up again.

"Professor Watkins." I tried not to blink or look away. I knew he was a Psychic but forgot what kind. "Hi." Ideas about what to say flitted around my head like moths around a porch light.

"Phillips. You and Adler have an interesting collection of information between the two of you." He stroked his salt and pepper goatee. "Interesting in the Confucian sense."

"Er. Okay?" I would have made some excuse, cut and run, but I couldn't get up with Olivia in the way, and Watkins was blocking her.

"Professor, Nox and I have been working with a few other students on some local history since last semester," Olivia smiled, her big amber eyes blinking periodically as she spoke. "It's kind of a fun thing we got together and did once we realized a bunch of us aren't from around here."

"Ah. You'd better not try to tell me either of you is the ringleader of this little project because I'd sooner buy the Newport Bridge than that idea."

"No way. It was Blaine Harcourt's idea originally." Olivia's smile faded as Watkins ignored her, keeping his eyes on me.

"I see." He gave one curt nod. "The textbook's a little dry for an extracurricular project." Watkins pulled a small notebook out of his back pocket and the ubiquitous pencil from behind his ear. "Go to the library. Find Taki Waban. Check these books out." He jotted a list on the paper, graphite scratching in spidery script with no care for the blue lines. "Whatever you do, don't discuss them around Changelings. Read the one about shifter pack history first." He tore the paper off the pad, holding it out to me. "And by first, I mean directly. Do not pass the dining hall. Do not collect your lunch."

"Ooookay?" As soon as my fingers pinched the raggedy top of the list, Watkins let go of it and stalked back to the podium to collect his own things.

Olivia and I got out of there like a couple of bats out of a belfry when the guy at the bottom pulled the rope. We passed the dorm and crossed the street to the library. Olivia headed for the card catalog, but we didn't find any of the books listed in it. Same results when we tried the computer.

"He said to find Taki Waban." I glanced around but saw no sign of the old dragon shifter.

"You mean that new librarian?" Olivia shrugged. "Lynn says he knows nothing about the Library of Congress or even the Dewey Decimal system."

"I don't think that matters." I strode away from the computer, heading back toward the staff areas of the library. Behind me, I heard the patter of Olivia's ballet flats against the hardwood as she jogged to keep up.

At the end of the hall, a counter stood between us and a set of double doors, the kind that swung either way and had little round windows in them at head height for everyone except Gnomes, Sprites, and Olivia. I peered through them, spotting motion way back near a stack of cardboard boxes. I thought I saw a head of black hair streaked with white.

"Mr. Waban?" I called out to him louder than usual library etiquette allowed. I didn't care. The book Watkins wanted me to read had something to do with wolf shifters. Maybe it could help Josh. I'd gotten him and his family into who knows what kind of trouble. I'd do anything I could to get them out of it. Apparently even risking the wrath of a dragon older than Blaine's mother, who'd come here with the Vikings.

"Miss Phillips. Miss Adler." The unassuming man pushed through the door, stepping up to the counter. "It seems Professor Watkins owes me fifty dollars. When he phoned, he told me to expect you at least half an hour from now."

"Well, he told us it was an emergency."

"He said no such thing to me." One corner of Mr. Waban's mouth tilted up in a half-grin. "However, he did go on for longer than I'd like about how none of his students know how to follow directions. So, it's an emergency now, is it?"

"Um." I'd blustered myself into a corner again. This seemed to be my new default mode since meeting Josh. I had the idea it didn't look good on me.

"Here, Mr. Waban." Olivia came to the rescue again, plucking the book list from my hand and passing it to the quasi-librarian. If only she didn't turn into a medically induced pumpkin at eight-thirty on the dot every night, she'd be a great person to have around through all this mess.

"Hmm. I've got two of these." Mr. Waban raised one eyebrow.

"Please tell me one is the shifter pack history book?" I put my now empty hands flat against the countertop.

"It is." He tilted his head. "But these books are part of my personal collection. They're not library copies. I could lend it to you, but I'd prefer it not leave campus."

"No problem. I'd prefer not to leave campus myself." I grinned.

"Excellent. Here you are." Mr. Waban pulled two books out from behind the counter, placing them between my hands. Both were bound in worn leather, wrapped around and tied with strong rawhide cord. They looked more like personal journals or a collection of research papers than anything published on a printing press.

"Thank you. I promise to have them back as soon as we're done." I picked the volumes up gently, tucking them together in the inside pocket of my jacket. Then, I turned and headed down the hallway.

"Very good." I glanced over my shoulder at the sound of his voice. His face was inscrutable, almost like a mask under a sheet of ice. "Please give Mr. Dennison my regards."

I just nodded, heading out into the cold bright sunlight of the winter midday. Then, I checked the time, realizing I had to meet Jeannie so I could get the keys to her room. I crossed the street to the dorm, almost forgetting Olivia was still following me.

"Go get lunch, my friend." After turning, I paused. "I'm room-sitting, remember? I have stuff to do in there."

"You catching a nap?" She blinked. If Olivia thought I needed one, I probably could use a full eight hours.

"Hopefully. After I talk to Jeannie."

"Okay, see you later." She opened the door for me, then trotted off toward the dining hall.

I stepped into the lobby. Jeannie came out from around the corner, beckoning to me. I followed her all the way down the hall to room 111. She opened the door to find a tidy single room. The bed had been stripped, but fresh linens were folded in a stack at its foot. The desk was clear, too. Jeannie yanked on the long handle of a suitcase with wheels, dragging it to the door. She handed me two keys on a ring with a tag that said I Love Boston. I'd almost forgotten that's where she was from.

"Thanks so much again, Jeannie."

"You don't have to thank me. Just rest and take care of yourself. I was where you are a long time ago, and someone helped my family and me." She shrugged. "Least I can do is pay it forward."

I'd never let anyone call Jeannie La Montagne a Barbie doll in my presence again. After she left, I went to work making the bed, then distributing some of my things around the room to make it more comfortable. I took off my pelt, placing it in the oilcloth. Then, I put that in my rucksack next to the desk. Just as I was about to sprawl out on the bed and crack open the shifter pack book, the buzzer went off. I wasn't sure how it worked, so I grabbed Jeannie's keyring and headed down the hall to the front door.

When Josh smiled at me through the wire-crossed glass, I tried not to let my knees knock together. I blinked, trying to remember whether I told him I'd be staying in Jeannie's room or not. A hot flash of jealous anger surged through my whole body, but I opened the door, anyway. Only the tightening of his jaw gave away the fact my mood was visible. At least I'd put away my pelt. I had a feeling Grandpa might have tried to drown him like he'd done with Tony.

"What's up, Nox?"

"Huh?" I strode down the hall, letting him follow me. I didn't want him seeing my face until I knew for sure he hadn't actually come here to see a busty blond bear shifter instead of me.

"Jeannie better still be letting you use her room, or I'll shave her head."

"How did you know?"

"What? That she's giving you a place to stay?" He stepped up his pace, so we walked side-by-side down the hall. "Olivia ran into me on the way from the dining hall. She thought maybe you'd want to see me."

"Oh, really?" I glanced at him from the corner of my eye. The fire in my belly cooled.

"Yeah, really. I think she's been reading too many romances lately." He chuckled. "Thinks she's a matchmaker or something."

"I saw a book by Jane Austen in her bag at class today." I stuck out my tongue.

"Could have been worse." He shrugged. "There's that best-selling book with the handcuffs on the cover.

"You really think someone like Olivia Adler would read mommy porn?" I shook my head.

"Why shouldn't she?" He actually winked, the sly dog.

"Well, she should if she wants to. I'd never." I leaned against the wall next to Jeannie's door, not quite ready to be alone behind a closed door with him yet. "But this is the twenty-first century."

"Girl's gotta get her kicks somehow, and I don't see anyone hanging around her door." He gave me a toothy grin. "Same can't be said for you." He put one hand on the wall above my shoulder, then leaned on it. Just as he bent his elbow to move closer, I stepped away, turning my back to him so I could open the door.

I headed in, standing in the middle of the room with my

hands on my hips. He'd gone in after me, of course, before I could say goodbye and shut the door which was the exact opposite of what I really wanted. I rolled my eyes, opening my mouth to say something snarkily reminiscent of Lynn. He covered it with his, wrapping his arms around me.

The way his body felt against mine was even more intense than the night before. How could that be when we weren't out in a semi-public place, and I had more on than an old blanket? Josh's hands moved up my back, one stopping across my shoulder blades and the other sliding up the back of my neck. He twined his hand in my hair, not pulling, but still holding firmly. He broke the kiss. I'd never have been able to. Somehow, I felt on fire and frozen solid at the same time.

The heat of his breath misted my cheek as he moved to the side and down to nuzzle my neck. I tried to say something, hoping maybe whatever words I'd utter might give me an idea of what this feeling was. No luck. The only sound out of my mouth was a breathy moan. This was ridiculous. I'd been there and done that, even if it was all the way back with my High School boyfriend. Of course, that was ancient history. I hadn't even looked at a man since Dad died and left me with the pelt way too soon.

If this had been a fight, I would have had the upper hand. Any move he made, I'd react with the counter, know where to look in order to anticipate his actions. I could do nothing but shudder. It was like the rest of the world went away. The only thing that existed besides me was him.

That probably sounds more romantic than Olivia's recent reading material. It might have been for someone else. I'm used to hearing eleven voices in my head and sensing magic in everything. I couldn't move. Nothing was in context anymore with the rest of the world on vacation.

Josh sensed this somehow. He pulled back, still cradling me against him, then ushered me to the edge of the bed. He pulled the chair out from under the desk, turned it around, and sat on it like a normal person instead of backward, for once. He leaned forward, putting his elbows on his thighs and resting his head on folded hands. Even though his posture was the height of informality, his face wore an expression of deep concern. I'd expected a million questions, possibly some kind of outburst driven by wounded pride. He said nothing, just sat and let me collect myself.

"That's it. Of course." I stood up on shaky legs. "Collect myself. Of course. That's why this isn't working. How stupid could I be?"

He cocked his head to one side, watching as I crossed the room to the desk. He still looked puzzled when I opened my bag. After I retrieved the oilcloth and put on my pelt, his eyes glimmered with a hint of understanding. I turned to face him, finally feeling ready for something other than a fight. I didn't waste time wondering whether it had been stupid to use it. Only what happened next could answer that question.

"You weren't really yourself either time then, huh?" He looked up at me, comprehension in his expression.

"Nope." I smiled. "Am now." A little thrill of anticipation shivered up my spine. The nearly numb tingle left over from his earlier caresses ran swiftly from cold to hot. It was my turn to chuckle now. I shook my head, sensing the approval and then slow retreat of my ancestors. Even Grandpa quieted, the stormy force of his personality calming to leave me with more control over the pelt's powers than I'd ever experienced.

It only took a few steps to cross the distance between us. Josh sat up, gathering his legs under him as he prepared to stand. I didn't let him. Instead, I reached down and tilted his chin up. Then, I planted one on him. A kiss, of course. He reached up, and I let him pull me down against him.

Later, when I pulled the borrowed sheet up to cover us, I heard the murmur of a twelfth voice, the song it sang familiar and sorely missed. Dad. Everything but the piece of him that'd live in the pelt had moved on. My eyes closed, heavy with profound relief and weariness.

"We were right," I managed. Then, I followed Josh's even breath under the surface of consciousness.

CHAPTER THIRTEEN

Josh

Pins and needles in my arm woke me up. I blinked, then tilted my head so I could kiss the top of Nox's head. She'd completely shocked me by rocking my world half the night like that. I smirked, remembering how awkward a kid I'd been before my first shift. I should have realized that without her pelt, she wasn't her whole self. I'd met Magi who'd lost their powers before, from encounters with Spites. If she lost her pelt, Nox would lose part of herself just like those Magi.

Now I'd have to find that drunk asshole Selkie's pelt or die trying. Literally, because she'd been right just before she fell asleep. Our hunches had been correct. This was righter than anything had ever been before in my life. I wouldn't tolerate anyone turning my mate into a shell of herself, not even the Sidhe Queen. I guess I'd finally taken a side, chosen a Faerie Court after all. I huffed out a little laugh.

It should have felt more like a major fail. It didn't. Even

though I'd been like a second spare tire in the family hierarchy, neutrality had been hammered so hard into Derek's and Beth's heads I couldn't have escaped the idea if I'd wanted to. Dad always said taking a side would mean betraying the trust people placed in wolf shifters. We'd been the first shifters in general law enforcement positions after the Big Reveal, so the pressure was higher on our family to work harder, be more upstanding than others.

But Mom always said it was even bigger than that. Taking one side weakened the other. An imbalance could tip the scales toward the first open Extrahuman war ever. But something always bothered me about that idea. Sometimes, conflict happened. You couldn't avoid it all the time, no matter how hard you tried. Someone somewhere wanted to screw things up until all the hard work and impeccable standards in the world couldn't prevent a fight. And that's exactly what was happening right here and now.

The Extramagus was smart. He or she knew that more young Changelings tithed to the King since the Big Reveal because the old rules Seelies had to follow didn't work in the new mingled world. The Kings Court grew while hers stayed the same. That Extramagus knew the Queen had more to lose if, say, a Spite got defeated and destroyed in combat, or a Selkie pelt went missing. Or the mortal police force aligned with the Unseelies.

But then, there was coincidence to worry about. I had no idea what Derek's mate might have been like as he hadn't told us about one before he'd gone missing. Beth had happened to make a nice appropriate match, but then he'd also gone missing. Was it my turn to disappear, or worse? Or did coincidence make things for Pack Dennison hard this time around because my mate happened to be Unseelie? Should I be waiting for some kind of accident? I shuddered.

"Okay." Nox wrapped her arms around me, holding me closer.

One of her hands reached up to stroke my cheek. "We got this. Whatever it is."

"Might be coincidence calling in its marker." I sighed. "Whammied both my siblings. Still think we got this?"

"Yeah, actually." She sat up, beaming at me in the morning light. Her black hair stood out against one pale shoulder, and a defiant twinkle lit her blue eyes like moonlight on water. "If Tinfoil Hat's Beta can give coincidence a one-finger salute, so can its Alpha."

"Thanks. I needed a magic horse shifter to encourage me to buck the odds." I winked. She laughed, then leaned down. When her lips met mine, my wolf surged forward in complete agreement with my state of arousal. I turned the tables on her, getting the upper hand in this round more handily than I'd done when we sparred at the dojo. The thought of what a challenging opponent she'd been just made me want her more.

The knock and music of female voices out in the hall was worse at that moment than taking the ice-bucket challenge. I groaned, getting up to grab my clothes and pull them on. Being a shifter had at least given me years of practice in getting decent quickly. Nox was right behind me, but slower. I smoothed out the bed while she went to the door.

"Who is it?" Her voice was higher-pitched than usual, the only indication I got that she might be as frustrated as I was just then.

"We're going for breakfast. Come on already, or I'll force choke you through the door."

"Okay, Darth Lynn." Nox peered in the mirror next to the door, detangling her hair with her fingers. "Give me a minute. Meet you at the front door."

"One minute, or Alderaan gets it." Lynn's quip faded, along with some giggling accompaniment that sounded like Maddie the Umbral Magus. Yeah, I remembered her. She was a packmate, which Alphas never forget. Kind of convenient that she was dating the Beta.

"Look, Nox. We still need to talk about what's happening on Monday. I made a promise to, um, your lawyer." I leaned one elbow on the wall next to the door and stuck the other out, scratching the back of my head. One glimpse in the mirror on the closet door put an end to that. No self-respecting guy wants to look like the awkward anime character trying to talk to his girlfriend.

"Yeah. Can you do it in a minute?"

"Talking, maybe. Anything else…" I shrugged and dropped her a wink. Nox threw back her head and laughed.

"Okay. I didn't much care about Alderaan anyway." Her smile made my breath catch in my throat.

"Look, at the end, when I win the match against Uncle Jake, I can't just trade you away to the Queen."

"But you have to." She crossed her arms over her chest. "That's the only way to make up for what I did."

"No. I don't have to. I'm going to refuse to order you around on this as either your Alpha or your mate." I tucked my chin, gazing into her eyes, fighting the urge to get lost in that bright steely blue. "I can't do anything but give an honest account of events and then leave it up to you."

"I don't understand."

"I'll explain it as best I can, then." I put my hands on her shoulders. "If I give in to the Queen, just hand over one of my most accomplished pack members who also happens to be my mate, I'll look like I'm siding with her. Wolf shifters mate. We have to, or we go nuts and can't be leaders. Someone as old as the Sidhe fricking Queen can't pretend to be ignorant about that. Coincidence makes mates, not Faerie or pack politics. If I roll over for her, I look weak. That and I couldn't live with myself if I cuffed you and handed you over like you did something wrong instead of being a hero. So, that's why it's going to be up to you. You go with her willingly, of your own volition and under your own power, or not at all."

"So you're letting me decide whether to stand trial?"

"Yup."

She closed her eyes, nodding. I smelled salt before I saw the glimmers at the corners of her eyes. When she opened them, a matched set of tears rolled down. Her lips parted, teeth stark and bared in a flavor of defiance I'd never seen before. She raised her hands to her shoulders, placing them firmly over mine. I'd shaken the hands of probably half the politicians, law enforcement officials, and society heads in the state of Rhode Island. None of them had possessed even half the strong confidence in Nox's grip.

"Then after you beat your jerk of an uncle, I'll turn myself in. Let the Sidhe fricking Queen figure out what to do about a Kelpie with a Tanuki lawyer." She closed her lips, letting them meet as she leaned in to press them quickly but firmly against mine.

If only that was how it went.

CHAPTER FOURTEEN

Josh

I met my pack on Monday an hour after sundown on the bridge near the Temple to Music in Roger Williams Park. They'd all had a look at Nox's local shifter history books over the weekend. Extrahuman affairs that had to be settled in front of an audience usually happened there. A crowd had already gathered. I spotted all the guys in the Night Creatures, plus Jeannie, Mr. Ichiro, and Kimiko. A smoky whisper from Blaine confirmed my suspicion that Taki Waban had shown up as well.

Henry pointed out the Redford family sitting far away from Albert the Sidhe Changeling. Maddie and Lynn put their hands to their cheeks at almost the same time when they spied Headmistress Thurston. Bobby scratched his head, then pointed out Professor Watkins next to a decrepit guy in a black Greek fisherman's cap, but when I blinked, the professor was alone again. Tony jerked his chin at Bianca the Medium. Pretty much everyone from PPC had shown. I didn't let it go to my head, though. The campus loved my dad.

And then I saw him. He and my mom were up on the dais, chained to one of the columns by shiny manacles around their wrists. My wolf snarled deep within, and I had to fight back hard to keep him from taking over. They'd used silver. Beth must have known and decided not to tell me because she knew how I'd react. Chaining a wolf shifter with silver, even something silver-plated, was pure torture. I'd always thought Uncle Jake had been kind of an asshole, but I'd never believed he'd do something that heinous.

A cool hand on my shoulder settled me for the moment. I didn't have to look; I knew the feel of Nox's hand by heart already. I nodded at her, then took a step forward and put my hands on my hips.

"Let's do this." I walked down off the bridge and down the gentle slope designed to let voices carry. The rest of Tinfoil Hat followed. Well, everyone except Olivia. She'd fallen asleep in the Harcourt family party bus on the way over from campus, the poor thing.

Everyone else stopped at the curved line in the grass that marked the division between the seats and the flat expanse of lawn in front of the white marble temple. I crossed it, continuing on until I stood in front of Uncle Jake in the middle. The mutineers, about two-thirds of the members of Mom's pack and a little less of Dad's, stood on the steps between my parents and me. I glanced over to see Beth hobble out of the audience and stand between Bobby and Blaine. The dragon shifter offered her his arm and she took it, somehow managing to look more like a girl posing for her senior prom picture than a woman who needed assistance to make up for the ill-fitting prosthetic on her missing leg. She caught my eye, and I nodded. If I couldn't beat Uncle Jake, she'd step up. It'd be a long shot, but if I injured him badly enough, she just might do it. Her leg was less of a liability in wolf form.

"So, you actually showed up." Uncle Jake jerked his chin, sneering over my shoulder at my pack. "Nice crew. Too bad none of them can fight worth a damn."

"You know what they say about people who assume." I glared down at him, glad I'd ended up being taller than Mom's little brother, even if he did have nine years on me. "None of them will need to fight anyway. I'll beat you alone."

"No, you won't." Uncle Jake whistled. A statuesque redheaded woman dressed in a long, flowing robe stepped out of the pack behind him. "I'm invoking the trial of mates. Laila will be fighting tonight, against whatever psychic waif you have that passes for a mate these days." He eyed Lynn and Maddie.

"Awesome." I'd seen Laila fight before. She was savage, brutal, and exploited any weakness she could find. She also answered to a whistle. Nox would wipe the floor with her. Well, the grass, okay? You know what I mean.

I heard the sound of muddled murmurs carry across the lawn from my uncle's side as I turned on my heel and walked away. Yup, I put my back to Jake. From the low growl, he was the opposite of pleased. I walked right up to Maddie May, who still might have given Laila a run for her money considering her Umbral magic. Then, I held out my hand to Nox, who'd been standing behind her.

I turned around, heading back the way I'd come, hand in hand with my mate. She stood half a head taller than Laila, although she was thinner. Nox's smile was nothing nice when she turned it first to Laila, then to Uncle Jake. A clammy chill emanated from her as she locked gazes with the man trying to usurp my parents.

"So this is your Uncle Jake?" Nox raised an eyebrow. "I thought the trial of mates was intended for use by pregnant female Alphas, Josh." By addressing me instead of my uncle, Nox's statement couldn't be taken as a direct challenge.

"Yup." I shrugged. "Mom did it last time something like this happened. That was before I was born." I gave Uncle Jake my best smile.

"No more ignorant questions from the human peanut gallery." Jake's lip curled up in a more severe sneer than before. "I called the trial and named my champion. Name her already and let them start."

"Fine." I let go of Nox's hand, then turned to her and gave her a slight bow. "This is a veteran member of my pack and my mate. You might have heard of her since she's a little bit infamous right now. I present the Kelpie, Nox Phillips."

Nox

There was no way I'd beat Laila, even though I'd spent half the weekend reading the local shifter history book. All the same, when Josh introduced me, I waved to the crowd. This wasn't my first public fight. Most of the Cherry Blossom School's trophies belonged to me, after all. Then again, that was before I became an Extrahuman.

I'd expected a reaction from both packs and the crowd in general, but nothing like what happened. A few boos started up behind Uncle Jake, but then an eerie trilling sound rose from Bobby Tremain's throat. Was it a Rebel Yell? It didn't matter. The moment of silence that followed it gave Tinfoil Hat time to start a huge cheer. Everyone in the general audience joined in, hollering their approval far and away beyond any low sounds of dissent. I even saw Headmistress Thurston with her fingers in her mouth, whistling.

I bowed to Laila just like Ren had taught me to do before any fight, and the cheers got more intense. Then I nodded at Josh. He took a step backward. Uncle Jake mirrored him. They backed away from the center of the lawn, leaving Laila and me facing each other on the dewy lawn.

We circled each other, and before I knew it, I'd cracked my knuckles. Stupid habit, but knowing I only had a ghost of a chance to win this duel had me on edge. At least it looked like Laila intended to start the fight in human form. I'd have to beat her fast, then, before she shifted. Shifting to horse form on dry land would weaken my magic. I couldn't spare a glance at the pond on the other side of the Temple to Music. If only this match had been over there, I'd be able to throw water spells around, along with my meager glamour.

I kept my gaze fixed on the space between my opponent's eyes, just like I'd been taught. That was why I missed it when she started shifting. By the time I realized what was happening, Laila's robe was a pile of gray fabric on the ground, and her face was the last human-looking feature she possessed. I murmured a few words of focus under my breath, hoping to cover my late shift with the illusion it was farther along. It didn't work. Laila clearly had some experience with Changeling or even Faerie opponents and the fact she hadn't moved yet meant the ephemeral shimmer of any Glamour had given me away.

Laila bolted forward, her head down. She faked left, then headed around me to the right. I'd just leaned all my weight forward to kick out with my hind legs when I felt the air of her passage under them. She'd been about to hamstring me. My nostrils flared as I blew out a misty breath in the chill night air. The half-moonlight silvered Laila's russet fur as she darted past on my left. I planted my feet, not daring to rear. She was fast enough to go for my gut before I could strike out with my hooves. Instead, I focused my energy on calling up the deeps.

The earth under me had moisture in the soil. I felt water slick my coat, drenching my mane and tail until they stuck to me. Laila snorted, clearly aware of what I was doing but not why. It took too much time for me to call water even at this short distance in horse form. The fact that some force in the shadows up on the dais pushed against my magic like Sisyphus's boulder made it all worse.

Laila circled me again, and I had to choose between countering her and continuing my spell. Slashes of pain crossed my back legs, throbbing as they buckled under me. I managed to prop my weight on my forelegs long enough to level a glare at my opponent, screaming out a defiant neigh as I unleashed the force of pent-up water directly at her muzzle.

She couldn't howl, bark, whine, or whimper. She couldn't breathe, of course, unless wolves had evolved gills. They hadn't. She paced back and forth twice as though held captive behind iron bars instead of an open lawn. Then, Laila shook her head, bending it to the ground so she could rub her nose and mouth against the damp grass. I'd only sort of defeated her. I had to stay conscious, or she'd win In the trial of the mate, victory went to the last shifter standing.

She'd cut my legs deeper than I'd thought. My head spun with magical effort and pain. The coppery scent of blood only made it worse until I glanced over at Josh. His fists clenched, and his arms shook. I let my gaze travel up to his face, wanting that to be the last thing I saw if passing out was inevitable. Renewed energy surged through me as our eyes met, either the fact of his love or the magical bond between us letting me dig deeper for more. Laila hadn't bothered looking back at Jake. My magic told me she'd waited too long before she slumped to the grass, her body slowly transitioning from wolf to human form as her body involuntarily tried to dislodge the water.

I called back my magic, letting go of the cohesive force damming up her airway. Water flowed from her nose and mouth. I dragged myself forward, tilting my head to listen for her breathing. It was slow, but even. I'd won. Shutting my eyes, I rested my now-hairless face against the cool, dank grass. I couldn't stand, so I wouldn't bother trying. A collection of hushed gasps from everyone but Uncle Jake's pack reminded me I was in the altogether. I hadn't worn a robe either, so one of my favorite outfits currently decorated the blood- and water-smeared battleground in tatters.

Something warm, dry, and slightly scratchy covered my back. A pair of long-fingered hands I'd recognize anywhere stroked my hair. A set of lighter footsteps squelched through the muddy grass behind me, and I felt a sting of antiseptic, then someone bandaging my legs.

"Don't turn her." Lynn always sounded bossy, but this time, her voice was tinged with concern. "The cuts are deep. I have to put a poultice and bandage on these. Even with her pelt, they might take a few hours to heal."

"Fine." Josh's voice was hushed and a little shaky. "Just hurry it up. She's coming."

I looked up, turning my head away from the suddenly solemn audience. At the top of the dais, Josh's parents stood rubbing their unchained wrists. That would have been nice to see, except for the presence of the person who'd freed them. I averted my eyes, but it was too late. They'd met hers.

"So this is the insolent scion of House Phillips." The Sidhe Queen's voice was lower-pitched than I'd expected, its vowels extended in a languidly musical drawl. She tilted her head, peering down at Josh. "Hand her over, young Alpha, or risk my displeasure."

"I'll do no such thing." Josh rose. Even though he was one of the tallest people I knew, he still had to look up to meet her gaze.

"Did you misspeak?" The Queen's sky blue gown somehow managed to make her figure look fashionably thin and lush at the same time.

"No, Your Highness." Josh stood as still as he had that night in the Memorial Grove, all his attention focused. "Nox isn't mine to hand over. She's done nothing to displease me either as a member of my pack or my mate. In fact, she saved my Beta's life and now has claimed this victory that freed my parents. She will go to face your justice of her own will or not at all."

"And does she realize what sort of catastrophe refusal will assure?" The Queen raised one amber eyebrow.

"She does." I propped myself up on my elbows, continuing the Queen's disregard for my presence by referring to myself in the second person. "And that's why she's agreeing to go with you as soon as her other packmate finishes tending her wounds." Lynn had a suspiciously sudden coughing fit, then finished taping the bandages to my calves.

"So, you agree to submit yourself to the custody of my guards immediately and surrender your pelt?"

"I'll let you imprison me, sure. But you can't have my pelt."

"I can't allow a prisoner to keep such a powerful magical item while in custody."

"That's okay." I glanced back toward the audience where Taki Waban sat. The left corner of his mouth tilted up, and he gave me a slight nod. "I've got a church-key. I'll use that to store it before you bring me in."

Before I could ask Josh to go back to the bus and get my pack, Blaine stepped forward, one strap slung over his shoulder. I hadn't seen him leave, but that was what he must have done when it was clear I'd won the match. He approached as Lynn went back to stand with Bobby, helping him support Beth.

"Here you go, horsefeathers," Blaine grinned down at Josh and me. "Now, all you need is a door and someone trustworthy to leave that key with."

"I could leave it with Ichiro-san." I winced as my attempt to get up filled with fail. "He's representing me." The pack hit the dirt near my head. I rummaged inside, pulling out a warm sweater and a cozy maxi skirt. I pulled them on as best as I could under the blanket draped over me.

"I've got an appropriate custodian in mind already." The

Queen clapped her hands. "Hertha!" Blaine's eyes widened. A steady but small stream of smoke wafted out of his nose.

I didn't look up. All I saw were a pair of red and black patent Christian Louboutin pumps step lightly over the grass, stopping in front of me. I rolled on my side, trying not to bend my knees. A tall woman with hair as black and polished as obsidian looked down her nose at me. She couldn't help it, really. It was the angle her head happened to be at when she bowed to the Sidhe Queen.

"My husband will convey you to my vehicle because it seems my son also has a conflict of interest in this matter." One of the woman's perfectly shaped eyebrows tilted as she scrutinized me. "The key will be safe in my hoard until the conclusion of the trial. I will see it delivered to the right party personally when the time comes." She directed her gaze to Blaine, eyes narrowing. "And we have a great deal to talk about once this is done, whelp."

I blinked. The Queen's clap had summoned none other than Hertha Harcourt, the most influential dragon shifter on the Eastern Seaboard. I knew the Queen ranked amongst the most powerful beings on the planet, but it hadn't really hit home before how dangerous defying her had been. I'd kind of just done it in the moment, only thinking about my friends and pitying that poor Spite. Finally, I understood exactly how screwed I was.

Mr. Harcourt held his hands palm up. I watched powder-blue scales cover them. He pointed the fingertips at me, blowing gently. I rose off the ground, carried by his Air magic as he strode to the limousine I'd ridden in with Maddie less than a month before. It beat trying to walk hamstrung.

I used the church-key on the passenger door, pulling off my pelt and sealing it in the oilcloth from my pack. Josh had followed us, and Mr. Harcourt must have had some compassion for young love, despite his emotionless facade. He stepped far enough away for us to have a few moments alone.

"Nox, I don't know what to say. I'll get you out of this."

"You can't. Nothing but information can help now. The

Queen has trials with law and order, not by combat like your pack. That's the King's way, not hers."

"Information's exactly what I'm banking on." He grinned. "I've still got a question to ask a certain ex-Spite."

"You shouldn't use that for me." I shook my head. "Save it for a time when you really need it."

"Believe me, this is the right time." He put his arms around me, holding me as closely as the Air magic would allow. "I'll do anything in my power to save you."

"You shouldn't worry. She wants my pelt. After that, she'll let me go. You don't have to save me because I'll be fine. I might even be a better mate as a regular girl. Definitely more appropriate."

"I can't believe I'm hearing this after you just fought in the Trial of Mates for me. I love you, Nox Phillips. That includes all twelve ornery ancestors in that pelt of yours. I've done my homework. A piece of you is in there too, a piece that'll be missing the entire time you go without it. I'm not letting the Queen do that to you without a fight."

"But I told you, she doesn't fight with fang and claw."

"Even better. I like a challenge." He ran his fingers through my hair. "Just because I have fang and claw doesn't mean I can't learn to fight on her terms. I'm not giving up. Neither will Ichiro-san."

Mr. Harcourt cleared his throat. Josh gave me a quick kiss, then backed away a few paces before he turned and ran back to the rest of our pack. The magical air wafted me away, over toward the Temple the long way. I handed Mrs. Harcourt the key on the way, struck by how much neither she nor her husband resembled Blaine. As I prepared to be imprisoned at the Temple to Music for the night, I thought about what Josh had said. I hoped using the rebel sprite's last question was worth it. But even with recent insider information, how could Josh beat the Sidhe Queen herself at a game she'd been playing since the dawn of humanity?

CHAPTER FIFTEEN

Josh

Blaine's party bus dropped Lynn, Bobby, Tony, and Olivia back at the dorms. It took the rest of us back to my house, including my parents and Beth. My blood relations all went directly upstairs. I tried to catch the Ichiros before they left the park, but they'd gone while I was talking to Nox. Probably for the best, considering Mr. Ichiro's warnings about conflicts of interest.

I brought Blaine, Henry, and Maddie to the basement with me. The rec room was down there, complete with a bar. I needed a drink. I poured Jaeger over ice in three shot glasses, then used the boiling water tap to make Henry some Earl Gray. He peered at the wall behind me, then took down a bottle of Gosling's and tipped a shot in the cup.

"A Gunfire, huh?" Blaine sniffed, clinking the ice in his glass. "Haven't seen one of those since Grandpa visited Newport."

"Who drinks hot tea in the summer?"

"Air dragons."

"Ah. Well, that's odd. How did you end up Fire?"

"Well, he's my step-grandpa."

"Wait. Your dad's not your dad?"

"Not technically. Look, we have more important things to talk about than my home life." Blaine puffed out a smoke ring. "What are we going to do about Nox?"

"I have a few ideas, but we should talk before I pull the ace out of my sleeve." I headed over to the pool table in the middle of the room, turned, then leaned on it. "The Queen wants a Kelpie pelt to make up for losing a Selkie one. Trogdor here knows artifacts. I need to know what's comparable that we can offer her."

"Nothing." Blaine didn't have to check anything or even think before answering. "Well, the original Selkie pelt that got lost, or a different Kelpie's pelt. But those are so rare they're nearly priceless."

"So, I have one question I can ask an extremely knowledgeable creature. Should I ask where to get a Selkie's pelt?"

"No." Henry inhaled the vapor over his teacup. "I know who you're going to ask and they won't be able to tell you that."

"So what should I ask, then?"

"How about asking it to give you evidence to win the trial?" Maddie leaned on the bar. "There's nothing that says the question has to be tightly focused."

"The problem with that is there's no evidence to help us win." Henry sighed. "Nox is guilty as charged. She undid the enchantment and used a Seelie artifact to do it. What I don't understand is how she got that float in the first place when you had it, Blaine."

"See, that's the weird thing." Blaine sipped his Jaeger. "I blurted out the idea of using it like a moron. But she shouldn't have even seen it. My bag was closed, the float under other stuff. Somehow, it was sitting right on top of my backpack, outside it."

"I think that might be my fault." Maddie looked so down her

curls even drooped. "I sort of asked for help that night. I think I know who moved it."

"Look, you did what you had to do." Henry put his arm around her. "Neither of us would be here if you hadn't."

"What exactly happened, Maddie?"

"I made an oath to a Gnome. I owe them now because they helped our allies get the right things to the right place at the right time."

"Makes sense." I shrugged. "Gnomes have a weird time-space ability that only affects themselves and stuff right next to them. Tell on."

"So, I think maybe the whole thing's coincidental." Maddie leaned back against the bar next to Henry. "I asked Lynn to look up some history stuff about pelts to see what kind of pattern we might need to break."

"Good." I nodded. "She's on that now?"

"Yeah. She just had to help Olivia get in her room. Anyway, she'll text us with whatever she finds."

Just as I was about to ask Maddie what other information she had about the Gnome, I heard a soft pop behind me and felt eyes on the back of my head. I pushed off from the table, reaching over to grab my drink. It wasn't where it should be. I turned around slowly. A tiny creature in a tall, pointy and shabby hat pushed a ball toward me. Speak of the Gnome, and they shall appear. I realized the little bastard was positioning the eight ball, so I was behind it.

"You're trespassing on dangerous territory, Gnome." I put my hands on my hips.

"Just here to call in my favor from the Lady over there." The little twerp pointed at Maddie, then smiled brightly. Well, not exactly. They smiled like Jaws. Their mouth was full of shark's teeth.

"Great. Because we didn't need her help at all on this." The sour tang of Blaine's sarcasm rang out over my shoulder, along with the scent and sound of more Jaeger sloshing into his glass.

"Coincidence helps those who help themselves." The Gnome held out their hand. Maddie walked over to the table, sighing.

"I know, Gee. But now's not a good time." Maddie shook her head. "We've got a crisis on our hands here."

"That's why I need your help right now, Lady." The gnome blinked, their eyes glittering.

"Oh, I get it." I narrowed my eyes. "You're trying to make us fail. You must want this to happen."

"No, wolf lordling." They shook their head. "I need the Lady's help to fulfill another obligation. It's better for you and the Kelpie if she comes with me."

"This is bullshit." I held one hand over my head, about to swat that Gnome like a cockroach.

"You should trust him." Henry's hand circled my wrist like an icy manacle. "I've known Gee Nome for nine years, now. Their timing's impeccable and they've never made my situation worse even when they could have."

"You aren't me." I broke his grip but lowered my arm to my side. "But I wanted you as Beta for exactly that reason. I need as full an explanation as you can give me."

"I don't remember why Gee helps me, but they say that's because I ordered them not to mention it. Must be something to do with an event I'm not supposed to remember. Anyway, the entire time I've known them, they had metal teeth. Now they're shark. Something's changed in Gee's situation. If Gee says they need the help now, they mean it. And think about shark's teeth for a minute. What does that bring to mind?"

"The ocean." I let out a breath I hadn't realized I'd been holding. "The float. Selkies." I stared down at the gnome. "Fine. You take Maddie and get out of here. Do your thing."

Gee Nome giggled, clapping their hands as they hopped from

one foot to the other. Then, they snapped their fingers. They and Maddie vanished with a louder pop than before.

"I wonder what a Gnome needs an Umbral magus for, anyway." Blaine scratched his head. "Especially one powerful enough to Vanish a full-grown person."

"They weren't that powerful before." Henry shook his head.

"Guess he leveled up, then." Blaine sighed. "Anyway, we need to decide what to ask the ex-Spite. Let's write some ideas down." He got paper and a pen from the desk on the other side of the room, then brought it back to the bar and sat.

We worked on ideas for about an hour when Lynn sent a text. I turned on the TV, then used the remote to navigate away from all the streaming services and get to the Internet browser. The files Lynn had sent would be easier to share on the big screen. I selected the first one.

"Huh." Henry stepped forward, pointing to the date. "I remember hearing rumors about this. A Kelpie died with no relatives who could take the pelt. Why are all those spots blacked out?"

"Redacted records." I selected the next one, showing Henry more of the same. "Either someone in this case is still around, or someone pulled major strings to keep it covered."

"It says over there that the pelt got sent to an appropriate custodian for storage." Henry scratched his head. "That sounds familiar."

"It should, Memory Man." Blaine sighed, practically collapsing into the easy chair behind him. "The Queen said that about my mom."

"So this isn't your mom's first Kelpie pelt rodeo, huh?" I punched Blaine's shoulder. "Come on, man. It's actually a good thing you have an idea. Otherwise, all this black magic marker redaction crap would just be a dead end."

"No, it's not good. And it really is just an idea until I can check the hoard inventory." Blaine leaned his elbows on his knees and put his head in his hands.

"Wait. Let me look at the rest of the files Lynn sent." Henry held his hand out for the remote. I gave it to him. He scrolled through. "Okay, look. This one here, it's out of place. There's a missing page."

"Well, Lynn says she sent them all."

"Figures. She's thorough." Henry nodded. "But the missing page can only be the form that tells who has a claim on the item and where it is. Since that's gone, someone influential must have covered this up."

"Leaping Luna!" A surge of hope flooded my heart. "That means there's another pelt out there. If we had another church-key, we could switch them."

"So not only do you want me to check the hoard inventory, you want me to steal from it?" Blaine froze, the tension in his muscles making him look almost like a statue. "From my own mother?"

"Well, if this was your mate, wouldn't you do it?"

"That's kind of my point, Josh. She isn't my mate. She's yours." His narrowed eyes gleamed with some hard emotion. "You want a switcheroo, you do it."

"Look, we still don't even know if the pelt's there." Henry's levelheadedness came to the rescue again. "We also don't know if that's what the Queen's going to want. We need to call the Sprite, and Blaine needs to check the inventory before we even know what's probable. Why not start there?"

"Makes sense." I held out my right hand at Blaine. "I promise not to ask you to actually take anything from the hoard. But I have another idea. Just check the inventory while I talk to the Queen's angry ex-servant."

"Fine. I need a hardwired Internet connection, though."

"Sure, no problem." I showed him the modem, and he plugged in.

Henry murmured something under his breath. A few moments later, a short, lanky figure crawled out from under the pool table. Unlike most others of its kind, this Sprite had lines around their eyes and extra hollowness below the cheekbones. The biggest difference was their wings. The bones were there, but only tattered remnants hung where bright windows should have been.

"The Son of Dennis wishes to ask his final question?" The Sprite peered up at me, then glanced at Henry and nodded.

"Yes. You know how the Queen has Nox. She's going to put her on trial, and she's going to be guilty."

"I know. I also know the Tanuki is her solicitor."

"Yup. So, in light of all that, what's the Queen going to sentence Nox with?"

"An enchantment of equal importance to the one she broke." The Sprite sighed, shaking their head. "For a Kelpie, that would mean she must surrender a pelt. She's lucky she's not Psychic or human. Otherwise, it'd be her life."

"I can't believe Ichiro couldn't get the charges dropped or negotiate something else."

"The Queen doesn't drop charges."

"Nox is my mate. I have to do whatever I can to save her."

"She will be saved. She will walk away from the trial alive."

"No, she'll only be half-alive without that pelt."

"Alive all the same," the Sprite fluttered one hand at their ruined wings.

"I understand." I sighed. "But that's not good enough for me."

"Wait. The lemon-lime soda said something interesting." Blaine looked over his shoulder. "The Queen will demand *a* pelt. Not Nox's, specifically. You don't have to do anything secret about switching it. It'd be totally in the rules to give her a different one. The Queen couldn't complain. And yeah, the one from the form is in the hoard all right. All I have to do is convince my mom to hand that one over instead of Nox's. She hates how the Queen orders her around. I bet she'd help just to stick it to her."

"Hey now, wait a minute." Henry shook his head. "There's one thing we didn't think about in all this. What about the actual owners of that other pelt? Are they around somewhere? I mean, we can't tell from all these redacted documents."

"If giving the pelt to the Queen would save Maddie, would you do it?"

"Not if that meant some other family would lose what's rightfully theirs. Maddie wouldn't stand for that sort of thing. Do you think Nox would?"

I sighed, at an impasse. I looked from Henry, the angel on my shoulder, to devilish Blaine. Both sets of eyes pleaded with me to do what each considered the right thing. I tapped one foot on the indoor-outdoor carpeting, unable to decide. I reached into my pocket, intending to just flip a coin and let luck decide. My phone buzzed. I flipped it over to find a message from a number I'd never seen before. I opened it.

Need help? ~K The end of the message was a string of emoji I couldn't decipher.

"What's this say?" I handed the phone to Blaine because Henry had a snowball's chance in Hell of translating that.

"Huh." Blaine smirked. "Is this K person a Psychic or something? Dog, bat, fire, an airplane and a castle on one line. After that, fangs, paper, a white house, an angel, and a raccoon." He handed the phone back. "They'd better be Psychic, or I'll think your basement's bugged."

"Nope, Tanuki." I pulled the quarter I no longer had to use from my pocket. "I was just about to flip this to decide things. Luck."

"Well, that explains a lot." Henry nodded. "All this was fallout from that lucky float. Blaine found it. I touched it, Nox used it. Your friend K must have been at the Temple tonight. I say we follow her instructions."

"Even though she's telling Blaine and me to head over to Newport and you to meet her about a paper?"

"I trusted Luck before, and it turned out for me. I'll trust it again." Henry let his arms drop to his sides, though his forehead was still all furrowed. "If she's got proof the family attached to that other pelt is all gone, no one can object to us letting the Queen have it."

"Look, man, if we had more time I'd wait until you verified it." I shook my head. "But Tanuki know what they're doing. If she says we have to work on things at the same time, then that's how we should play it."

"But aren't Tanuki supposed to be kinda shady?" Blaine raised an eyebrow. "I mean, I really want to see my mom get off her designer couch and actually do something for a change, but is this particular gal one we should trust?"

"You know the lawyer representing Nox?" Henry waited until Blaine nodded. "She's his daughter. Annoying, but I think she genuinely wants to help."

"If it's good enough for the dead guy, it's good enough for me."

"That's undead to you, Trogdor." Henry gave Blaine a sideways look. Then, they both chuckled. "Okay, let's get out of here. Where am I supposed to meet this Tanuki?"

"Her dad's house." I scrawled an address on a napkin, knowing how navigating by smartphones was a bitch for vampires. "That's what the house and the angel meant. It's on Angell Street. Let's head out."

Henry took the napkin and followed Blaine and me out the door that led to the side of the house. The vampire amped up his speed with blood, heading around the house and out of sight in a breath. Blaine and I walked at a more sedate pace toward the expanse of grass at the back of my family's property.

"Is this enough room?" I eyed the space. We used to play soccer on it back when Derek and Beth were still in High School. I had no idea how big Blaine was in dragon form.

"It'll do." He puffed out a smoke ring. "You'd better get in front of me, though."

I stepped around and turned my back. Instead of the expected rustle of fabric to indicate he'd disrobed, I heard a series of rips and pops. The rich ass bastard had just shredded his clothes shifting. I could have afforded that myself, but never did unless it was a huge emergency. The Harcourts sure seemed to have brought Blaine up with weird priorities.

I turned around to see a red and orange scaled reptilian face staring back at me with red eyes and vertical pupils. He jerked one thumb-like claw at a spot on his neck. Pretty obvious he wanted me to get up there and hang on all the way to Newport. I wasn't sure I liked the idea of freezing, but when I climbed on, I was surprised to find his leathery skin hot to the touch, like someone with a high fever. I remembered something from class about dragon shifters not actually being reptiles, more like echidna and the platypus. Before I could recall it all, Blaine leapt into the air.

It was easy enough for me while he ascended. That seemed to take forever and felt like gravity had a hand pressing down on my back. During the descent, the wind tried to knock me off like I was on the ropes at a Royal Rumble. I felt movement behind me as Blaine tilted his wings. We coasted, and the wind resistance got more tolerable. Still, by the time we landed, my nails were blunted, my shoulders stiff, and my knuckles white.

The outside of the Harcourt mansion was white marble, all lit up with floodlights. Blaine had landed near a gazebo. I turned when he shifted, waiting until I heard a hollow *thunk* of wood followed by rustling fabric. When I turned around, he was fully dressed and already striding across the lawn to the house. I shrugged and followed, ignoring the rudeness. At least it wasn't like I'd need directions or anything. The mansion was obvious.

The entrance was even more ostentatious than the one at my house. Everything was huge, of course. Blaine could have gotten in without shifting if he'd really wanted to, though everyone in the house would have heard him coming. As it was, I made more noise than him, the soles of my combat boots a hollow counterpoint to the soft sound of his bare feet.

I swallowed, increasing my pace to catch up with him. I reached one hand out to his shoulder, about to stop him and call things off. Nox wouldn't be okay with what we were doing. Making a magical pelt, pieces of some other family's ancestors, pay the price for her own actions was something she might not want to do. I couldn't think of any reason the Sidhe Queen would want an Unseelie magical item unless she intended to destroy it. Nox wouldn't stand by and let that happen.

"Let me tell you a story," Blaine increased his pace, escaping my imminent grasp, "about a man and a woman very much in love."

"Huh?"

"Just shut up and listen, Beowulf." Blaine sighed. "Fine, I'll give you the purple-proseless version. The Queen and the King had a hard time making babies, so they adopted mortals to carry pieces of their power, passed down through generations by blood or trinket. That was where Selkies and Kelpies came from, along with a few other things long since extinct.

"But some mortals got powers of their own. The Queen governed with a strict hand and swift punishments. The King tested with guidelines and reinforcement. They fought, cut their kingdom in half. The King got custody of all the children who carried his magic, likewise for the Queen. But the grandchildren didn't always choose the same way, except the Selkies and the Kelpies."

"Okay, so that's why a Redcap or a Sidhe or a Goblin can choose courts and a Kelpie's always Unseelie."

"Yup. The pelts can't switch sides because the power's not genetic." Blaine sighed. "But all Faerie creatures are like kids to the monarchs, so she'd never destroy a Kelpie pelt. She'd just keep it."

"So this is more like a custody battle in a messy divorce than offering up a lamb to the slaughter?"

"Exactly." Blaine turned his head, raising an eyebrow. "Feel better?"

"Almost." I tapped the phone clipped to my belt. "I wish they'd find something and text."

"Look, nothing in this world is perfect." Blaine stopped, so I did, too. We faced each other in front of a door that could have been the side of a barn. "You find one perfect situation, everything else goes to hell so you don't take it for granted. Happened to Bobby and Lynn, Henry and Maddie. It's your turn, dog-man. Don't screw it up by failing to take a risk."

"But what if what I'm risking is Nox hating my guts?" I blinked a few times, clenching my jaw.

"Is the goal to get her to love you? Because I think you've got that covered. You're trying to keep her soul intact." It was Blaine's turn to blink. His eyes went red and reptilian, then faded back to their normal color. "At least, you'd better be."

"The Hell do you mean by that?"

"Do you care about her, or what she thinks of you?" Blaine's shoulders quivered slightly. I noticed he'd been clenching his fists. "Because you sound more like a dragon shifter than Alpha of the first pack to have a vampire alliance in umpteen years."

I glared, looking him right in the eye. Neither of us blinked. I reached out with my right arm, pushing against the door next to us. It opened a crack which for that door was enough space for us to walk in side by side.

"Let's go in there and tell your mom how awesome it'll be to stick it to the man with a switcheroo."

All the tension went out of Blaine's face, shoulders, and hands. He closed his eyes. Instead of relief, he looked exhausted. Worse than that, he reminded me of the time I'd seen a guy up on the

Pell Bridge, surrounded by EMTs and Firefighters trying to stop him from jumping. I felt a tug at my sleeve. The Sprite with the tattered wings stood there, peering at Blaine. It looked up at me, then nodded. I understood.

"You went in here all gung ho, and you knew." I shook my head. "You're going to put your mother up to this and put yourself right in the way of the Extramagus. No wonder you got so pissed when I hesitated."

"I can handle a puny mortal, Beowulf." The small noise he made wasn't exactly a snort. There wasn't even a trace of smoke around him. "I bet even Extramagi are crunchy and taste good with ketchup."

"Thank you." I didn't know what else to say.

"Shut up and let's do this already." Blaine turned, disappearing past the doorway. I followed him, struck once again by how my seemingly haphazard pack kept turning out to actually be made of some seriously impressive people.

CHAPTER SIXTEEN

Nox

The stone looked pastel blue in the morning light. It reminded me of veins under pale skin. I breathed in the dewy air, the scent and feel of the nearby pond in my lungs and on my skin. None of that would do me any good without my pelt, but the humidity gave me some small measure of comfort. I shivered, sharpening the dull ache of the wounds on the backs of my legs.

Something warm and soft moved away from my back. At the same time, three soft hoots came from somewhere above. I looked up into the eaves of the Temple to Music. Instead of pigeons as I expected, something white and shaped like a small barrel perched. I rubbed my eyes, and when I blinked again, it was gone. I glanced down to see a huge fluffy cat with tufted ears like a lynx's. Except this was no lynx. Its fur was black and glossier than most long-haired felines. It blinked bottle-green eyes at me.

"There's no way you're—" The cat hissed, cutting off the name

I'd been about to say. The tip of its tail flicked. It padded up beside me, bumping its head against my right front pocket. It sat, leveling a stare at the church-key in my pocket and then at the door to the electrical panel behind me. I glanced around. The Sprite guarding me was all the way down the steps, admiring the oncoming dawn. I'd never seen him shifted before, but I knew without a doubt that this was Tony, telling me to use the key and escape.

"No way," I whispered. "I won't run and hide for the rest of my life."

Tony's cat ears flicked, and he blinked. A flutter of wings and a single soft hoot came from the eaves again. Olivia? When Tony looked up and flicked his tail at me, I figured I was right.

"It's nice of you to visit and all, but the guard will be back soon." I waved the backs of my hands at them. "Now shoo."

They barely made any noise leaving. I wondered whose idea that had been, but it didn't matter. If the Queen had thought I'd use the third church-key, she'd have taken it from me. I'd agreed to imprisonment and the trial, and I wouldn't go back on my word. I didn't want to be punished, but if that was what happened, at least it was for something I'd done. People on trial in the mortal courts weren't always so lucky. I shuddered, thinking about Professor Brodsky. If the court couldn't find evidence he'd been mind-controlled, he could be executed for killing two vampires and attempting to murder a third. I hoped he didn't lose, and that the right criminal would be brought to justice.

No matter what happened today, I'd be losing something. If I was lucky, I'd walk away from this trial a Kelpie, but I couldn't be with Josh. If I was unlucky, I'd lose part of myself. At least Josh's parents couldn't object to us settling down. But I had to wonder what good that would be. I couldn't have accepted everything that went along with my magic if it wasn't for Josh. And I wasn't even sure I could be a proper mate to him without that missing piece. It wouldn't be right to make him settle for half a mate.

A hand, small and strangely padded, covered one of mine. I looked down to see something more like a paw, black, furry, but still five-fingered. Deep brown eyes glittered from a band of nearly black fur. A Tanuki. The first rays of the dawn touched the back of my hand, lighting the paw resting against it with a golden glimmer. I blinked, feeling a small but steady flicker of warmth around my hand. It traveled up my arm, so ticklish I had to use all my martial arts training to sit still and bear it.

"Ichiro-san?" But no. It couldn't be. This Tanuki's ruff was long and lush, with less silver in its coat than I'd ever heard of an older Tanuki having, even when they'd used Luck charms to gain more years of life. "Kimiko. What are you doing here?"

The young Tanuki cocked her head to one side. Her mouth opened in a canine grin as she removed her paw from my hand.

"Got it. You were never here." I chuckled. "Thanks for the visit." Josh had obviously found her annoying, but she must have had a big, brave heart to come all the way over here. I watched her trot away, the black-tipped bushy tail bobbing along behind her comical enough to make me chuckle again.

It felt colder when she left, despite the sun. I pulled the single woolen blanket the Queen had ordered left with me more tightly around my legs. That's when I noticed the little box sitting where Kimiko had been. It smelled like food. I wondered how she'd managed to bring an item with her and leave it behind without shifting, then remembered. Tanuki didn't have elemental magic. Their talents varied individually. She must be able to hide objects. I opened the box to find three rice balls. I wolfed them down before my Seelie guard could notice them.

On the bottom of the box was a message in black ink. I read it silently. *Trust your mate.* I blinked and read it again, wondering what I should do with it. That message might just make things worse for me if it got discovered. But the box shimmered and dissolved once the full light of the sun hit it.

"What are you doing?" I turned to see a familiar bundle of bamboo sticks crackling as they leaned over me.

"I could ask you the same thing. Where's the Sprite?" I glanced down the steps at where they'd been earlier. They were gone.

"None of your business. I told you we'd be meeting again that night at the Summoner's home."

"Yes, under very different circumstances if I remember correctly." I narrowed my eyes. "Are you here on the Queen's business or the Summoner's?"

"The Summoner couldn't hold me once he'd been captured. The mortal authorities broke all his anchors." I wasn't sure how a creature who looked like a stick-bug could sound smug, but this one managed.

"Well, here's to different circumstances." I raised a mock glass to the Brownie. "Maybe I have a chance of walking away from this."

"You do." They stiffened. "This too shall pass, but likely not in the way you'd expect."

"You Brownies and your fortune-cookie psychobabble." I rolled my eyes.

They ignored my taunt and stood rigid, their entire body straight as a sapling, which meant they had relaxed. The Brownie swayed a little in the breeze coming off the pond. I turned to look down the lawn. The first few cars pulled up to the curb nearest the Temple to Music. One of them was a Campus Police car, followed by a Providence Police cruiser and a Psychic News Network van.

"The News is here? Seriously?" I sighed.

Something clattered on the marble in front of me. A small white bottle with a red and white label. Tylenol. I peered back up at the Brownie. I had no idea whether they were looking in my direction or not. Even a bona fide tree hugger would know where to start with a Brownie. They looked more like mini Ents than little elves.

"What's this for?" I popped open the cap, finding the foil seal underneath still intact. They weren't trying to poison me, then.

"Mortal pain relief. You are both mortal and in pain, are you not?"

"No, I mean the kindness routine." I peered up, the sun making me squint. "What gives?"

"You were wrong to undo the Spite, but if you and your friends hadn't investigated the Summoner, I'd still be his slave." It creaked and crackled a bit. "Giving you something of his is customary. After all, you defeated him. That means you are entitled to some spoils by our laws."

"Analgesic spoils." I snorted. "Any port in a storm." I rattled two pills out of the bottle, realized they weren't extra strength, and shook out two more. I dry-swallowed them.

Back at the curb, more vehicles had pulled up. It was going to be a long beginning to an unpredictable day.

CHAPTER SEVENTEEN

Josh

"I know why you're here." Mrs. Harcourt had her back to us, and still she had the upper hand. I wasn't surprised; this was her house, after all. "I noticed the item you searched for in the hoard database, Blaine."

Blaine put one finger to his lips, stopping at the end of the long hallway we'd walked down. I stood next to him in the doorway which was wider than the Thayer Trolley Tunnel back in Providence. The hall opened on a hexagonal room, something like a foyer by way of decoration. It was huge, just like the rest of the mansion. Dragons need their space, I guess. For a few moments, Blaine's mother arranged red-tipped purple roses in a vase. Then she turned around, a slight smile on her brick red lips.

"You have your dog friend well-trained, whelp." Mrs. Harcourt ignored me, walking toward her son. "Good. Maybe he can clean a mess up for me instead of making one like the Kelpie did."

"What did you have in mind, Mother?" Blaine's voice sounded completely different here than it did at school. Without the zing of sarcasm or nonchalant confidence, he sounded like a different person. I wasn't sure what to think of Newport Blaine.

"We've got a pest problem again." Mrs. Harcourt put a hand on one hip, leaning all her weight on the opposite foot. She didn't look much older than her son, but she was supposed to be from the tenth century or something. I tried not to get too creeped out by that.

"Oh, no." Blaine's hair flopped from side to side as he shook his head. "Not Pharaoh's Rats?"

"Nothing quite so dangerous." One corner of her mouth tilted up. "Only a cockatrice which is why I don't want you or your step-father taking care of this. I'll brook no threat to my husband's manhood or my future grandchildren."

"Eww, Mom." Blaine's nose wrinkled. He reminded me of the time I was fifteen and got grossed out by catching my parents necking.

"I don't get it." I gave Mrs. Harcourt the same kind of smile my mom gave the District Attorney and the mayor. "Why can't a dragon shifter fight a cockatrice?"

"They're bad for the male's fertility." Her smile glittered with brittle humor. She reminded me of how Lynn was before she got together with Bobby. "I might be ages older than either of you, but I've got a husband for a reason."

Her statement would have made me more uncomfortable if she hadn't glanced at the portrait of a man on the far wall. I almost had to squint to see it was Blaine's step-dad. Another portrait hung to its left. The guy in that painting looked like my packmate. I didn't have to wonder where Blaine's bio-dad was. Dragons were possessive, so he had to be dead, or Mrs. Harcourt wouldn't have moved along to another man. The guy's clothing looked old, like something out of a Civil War flick. But how could Blaine be his kid if the last time he'd been painted was

1863 or whatever? I couldn't afford to think about that right then, so I dropped the thought. There'd be time later.

"I managed to lock the pest in here." Mrs. Harcourt's voice was coolly commanding, like someone who expected to be obeyed. "Head on in and don't come out until you have a dead cockatrice to show me." Mrs. Harcourt gestured to the door opposite the one we'd entered through, looking like a younger, raven-haired Vanna White. "I suggest you shift. They're fast, and they have sharp claws and beaks. And mind its gaze."

I stared at the door she'd gestured to, only aware she'd left the hexagonal foyer by the fading click of her heels. I stood next to Blaine, hoping he'd say something. This was his stomping ground, not mine. I waited as long as I could, then tapped my foot.

"What?" Blaine's voice was softer, tiny somehow compared to the larger-than-life mask he usually wore on campus.

"Give me the supernatural geek squad rundown." I turned to look at him. "I know how to chase chickens, but a cockatrice is only half one of those. So, what do I do?"

"I can't believe she asked you to do this." When he turned, I noticed his sweaty brow. His pallid face was set in an expression more uneasy than the one he'd worn before we came down here. How was that possible? "I'm so sorry."

"But I don't get why you should apologize." I shrugged out of my jacket, letting it fall with a hollow thud to the floor. Then I kicked off my boots.

"Don't let it scratch you. Its claws and beak have a venom that acts fast enough to be a mortal threat for a shifter your size. And don't look into its eyes." Blaine shuddered. "Look, maybe you shouldn't do this. Maybe Ichiro will talk the Queen down from taking Nox's pelt. Maybe I can stomp the thing, and we can tell Mom you did it."

"Nope. I'm not going to lie to Hertha Harcourt. And Yoshi Ichiro might be a legendary lawyer, but this is the Sidhe Queen we're talking about here. I can't take chances that aren't on me." I pulled my shirt over my head. "When you find your mate, you'll understand."

"It won't matter when I do, but that's not important now." Blaine's lower lip trembled. Was he about to lose it or something? I couldn't fathom why. He turned his back before I could ask. "What's important is, don't meet its gaze. If you do, Mother will have a wolf statue to add to her hoard."

"You mean it can go Medusa on me?" I unbuckled my belt.

"Yeah. Not if it sees you. Only if you look it in the eye. That's going to be tough on your wolf." His shoulders shook. "I'm gonna ask you again not to do this."

"I'm gonna tell you again, I'm doing it." After I folded my pants, I put them on top of my jacket with my shirt.

"Last chance. Back out, Josh." Blaine sighed. "Mother made this sound like a cakewalk. It's not. She values that pelt, so she gave you a task you might not survive. You could get maimed worse than Beth. You could die. There's no coming back from getting turned to marble."

"I wonder if cockatrice tastes like chicken." I chuckled to cover up the fact that I didn't care whether I made it as long as Nox got to stay whole. "No more questions. I'm shifting." Joints bent, lining up for running on all fours. My skin itched as it stretched and sprouted gray fur. I shook my ruff, then stretched. My wolf was ready for a fight.

Blaine didn't say anything else. He ran both his hands over his head, then dropped them to his sides. I sat on my haunches, noticing there was a human-sized door-within-a-door. Blaine opened that, keeping his back to me. I leaped inside, letting him close the door fast behind me so the cockatrice wouldn't get out. He needn't have bothered. I only caught a trace of its scent, a feathery, leathery, wet-stone kind of smell, shot through with a faint rot that could only be the poison.

The room was full of glass-fronted bookcases, packed to the

gills with scrolls, clay tablets, marked hides, and books. At least I wasn't there to get rid of a bookworm infestation. The cockatrice's scent wasn't anything like the shelf contents. It was somewhere on the other side of the room from me, but the place was laid out in stacks. I guessed it was the Harcourt family library. Lynn would have given her left arm to get in here. Not with a cockatrice around, but still. They supposedly had stuff from ancient Roman times, maybe even earlier.

I heard the hushed chuckle of a cluck before I realized the little monster was atop the stacks. I swerved out of the way just in time. Three of its claws caught my fur, pulling a clump out. I decided not to look up or back, running around the shelving in a circle instead to try to get behind it. No dice. The next aisle of shelves was empty, the cockatrice already either back up top or over in a different row.

I trotted along, wishing I could velvet my claws like a panther or lion shifter. Even when I was careful, they made a noise on the floor. Why couldn't the Harcourts have carpet like normal people? Oh, right. Carpet was flammable. But so were books. Crazy dragons. I'd have to tell Blaine that if his family wanted wolf shifters hunting down their library pests, they should get softer flooring in here. A rug would really tie the room together.

This time, I felt the rush of air as the weird creature swooped down. I finally got a decent look at it. It had a long, green, reptilian tail I didn't expect, along with taloned claws more like an eagle's than a chicken. It was bigger than the average Rhode Island Red, too. The feathers I dared look at on its neck and breast were red and green, giving it an ironically cheery Christmas look. I jumped out of its way, but it almost pecked me. Instead of running down another aisle, I circled it. When I leaped, it fluttered back, tail dragging along the floor behind its skinny little bird legs.

I had no idea what it'd do next. The whole fight would have been easier if I could have looked at its eyes like I'd trained for, but that'd be fatal. The eyes might not have even shown me where it'd go next, anyway. I'd figured one thing out, though. That tail was a weakness. Its weight slowed the cockatrice down and probably didn't do it much good in the flying department.

It attempted to peck me again. This time, I cut the corner close when I went around it, going for the tail. My teeth sank into scaly flesh, piercing it and drawing blood. My wolf jaws were strong, and once I'd gotten my teeth in, I knew the fight would be over soon. Shaking my head, I knocked the cockatrice against one of the shelves. It let out a loud cluck, then a screech as I jerked my head the other way to slam the creature against the floor.

Growling, I dragged it back the way I'd come in, toward the door. It got hard to breathe with my mouth full of its blood. At least, that was what I thought. Each time it struggled, I shook the cockatrice again. Once at the door, I let its tail go. A sad-looking heap of scales and feathers sat at my feet. I sniffed it, found it still breathing. I took the back of its neck in my jaws and twisted. Once I felt the snap, I scratched at the door.

Blaine stood in the doorway, then sank to his knees on the threshold. His eyes were bloodshot, his face even paler than before. His hands shook as he fumbled a phone from his pocket. I heard gasping breaths as he tapped the screen, so why wasn't his chest heaving to go along with them? I fell on my side. Oh. That was my chest, my breaths.

"Tiamat's Scales, Josh." His voice was a hoarse near-whisper. "I told you to be careful." Blaine glanced at his phone, then reached out to touch my left front shoulder. He parted fur, peering. "A shallow scratch. Shards of the first egg, why did you do this?" He picked up the phone again, holding it out to snap a picture. Then he tapped the phone again, sending another message.

I whined, trying to get up, get out of the library on my own. I couldn't. My front legs wouldn't hold my weight. I pushed with my back legs, scooting myself along. Once my tail was out, I stopped. My tongue lolled from my mouth. Voices I could barely understand came from down the long hallway across the foyer, sounding like the time Beth and I tried to have a conversation through a box fan.

"Hang on, Josh." Blaine patted me on the head. On a better day, I would have bitten him for that, or was that a worse day? The last thing I remembered was the most important. I'd done it. I'd saved Nox.

CHAPTER EIGHTEEN

Nox

The cuts on the backs of my legs felt like a hundred wasp stings. That was actually an improvement. Before the Tylenol, they'd felt like a thousand wasp stings. My stomach grumbled despite the rice balls, and still I waited. The Brownie stood nearby as they had for the past two hours, like a tree. They hadn't said a word. I didn't blame them. The Queen had arrived shortly after the Psychic News Network van. She'd spent the entire time sitting in her magical levitating carriage, though.

I spotted Ichiro-san's car. He got out, juggling a briefcase, a drink tray, and a brown paper bag. Beth came around from the other side of the car to help him, without a crutch. A gust of wind pressed her trousers, outlining the brace that held her prosthetic on. She took Ichiro-san's briefcase and then his arm. Together, they approached me.

The length of time their walk took made me remember just how big the lawn in front of the Temple to Music was. I wondered whether as many people would show up here as there'd been last night. I almost lost my appetite. Fighting in front of a crowd was one thing, but being on trial made my gut feel like an entire flock of butterflies lived in there. Even worse, the Psychic News Network people were setting their cameras up at the top of the hill, like caretakers for insect-flamingo hybrids, the lenses like gaping, toothless mouths. That was worse than contemplating a crowd to stare and gasp at my guilt.

Ichiro-san and Beth sat, opening the bag which smelled like heaven and erased my awareness of the cameras for a while. I had donuts and coffee with them, trying to ignore the news crew and the people who steadily filled the lawn like an army of ants marching on a picnic. Waiting for this trial was worse than waking up hours before an exam I hadn't studied for. But, like an exam, its beginning would come on like the tide. Nothing I could do would stop it.

I'd almost forgotten the Brownie was still on the dais with us until they crackled a few times. At the foot of the steps, a rowan wood platform appeared with a clear crystal hovering in the air above it. Clicks sounded and flashes flickered in the crowd as the audience took pictures. I tried to swallow the lump in my throat. It wasn't just the Psychic News Network I'd have to worry about. I'd probably go viral on YouTube before noon. Not the way I'd always imagined becoming Internet famous.

"We'll head down there as soon as the Queen arrives." Ichiro-san patted my shoulder. "When she makes a statement, the truth crystal's color will change to reveal how honest your agreement is."

"So when she asks whether I undid the enchantment, I just say yes, and that's it?"

"Not exactly." He sighed. "You'll need to address her properly as 'Majesty' or 'Highness.' I have a list of questions here that she might ask you, depending on the crystal's reaction."

"Can you tell me what they are?"

"No. That'd make you automatically guilty of anything she thinks you might have done."

"Wow, that sucks." Beth blurted out what I'd been thinking. "Nothing like a mortal trial."

"Are you truly so surprised?"

"Someone should negotiate to change that." Beth shook her head.

"Plenty try to do just that, but in the opposite way you'd imagine." Ichiro-san sighed again. "Many mortals think the Queen's way is better. More reliable."

"That's insane." Beth sighed, shaking her head. "With Extrahumans in Law enforcement now, it's way easier to analyze evidence and arrest the right person."

"And also one of the reasons your Headmistress opened her school to anyone with the grades. Extrahuman Law is a major anyone can take, and since the Reveal, we need more lawyers with that kind of education. If only more humans would enroll."

"Wait for it," I grinned. "Lynn Frampton's a pretty good poster-child to attract that kind of student. Maybe I will be, too."

"Don't resign yourself to defeat." Ichiro-san opened his briefcase, removing a lapel pin. He took the backing off and pressed the point through the striped wool of his suit. Beth leaned a little closer, sniffing. The corners of her mouth turned up.

"Yeah, don't give up." Beth patted my arm. "It's Mr. Ichiro's job is to negotiate the sentencing in your favor. He's got some tricks." She glanced at the pin again. It was probably magic, but without my pelt, I couldn't tell for sure or get an idea of what kind.

"But I'm definitely guilty."

"And the Queen will enact the law to its letter. But sentences are flexible. Have hope." He affixed the back of the pin behind the lapel, then patted it.

"Yeah, I've heard that recently."

"Good." He stood, smoothing his suit. Then he nodded to the Brownie.

The sticklike creature guided me down the steps, one of their twiggy ends hooked in the three-link chain between my manacles. I stopped two paces behind them, next to the truth crystal platform. They let go, then stepped behind me. Ichiro-san stopped beside me. Beth went back to a chair on the lawn, next to Lynn, Bobby, and Olivia. A pair of empty seats made me wonder where Josh and Blaine were. I wanted to ask, but it was too late. The Queen stepped out of her carriage, gliding across on golden gossamer wings she'd kept folded the night before.

She wasn't alone this time either. A stream of Sidhe attendants trailed to each side of her. They moved together, synchronized like ballet dancers partnering their mirrored reflections. They arranged themselves prettily at the aisle points in the seating, but I wasn't fooled. These Sidhe didn't even have a Glamour up. Everyone could see their alabaster skin, pointed ears, white hair, longer-than-human limbs, the watchful glitter in rainbow eyes. Those who cared to check would note that the baubles at their wrists and ankles had blades, their earrings were hollow tubes, and their necklaces strung with elf-shot darts. These were militant guards, not showy attendants, and armed to the teeth.

The inside of my head was too quiet. I actually missed Grandpa's sound and fury. What would he think of all this? What about Dad? Would they call me foolish for risking them like this, or praise me for doing the right thing by owning my actions? The only way to find out was to get through this.

The Queen stopped opposite us. Unlike the other Sidhe, her hair was streaked with amber that matched her eyebrows. Whether that was natural or some cosmetic she used, no one knew. One of the attendant warriors flicked his wrist a few times, straightening the monarch's jet black gown. I wondered why she'd worn that color, then realized how it made her white skin stand out in stark contrast. Black and white, no gray. Seelie justice. I took a deep breath and let it out slowly.

"You are Nox Phillips." The Queen's voice was quiet but commanding.

"Yes, Your Highness." A faint trace of gray formed at the center of the crystal. I closed my eyes. Of course. I should have said no and stated my full name. I opened my eyes. "No, Highness. My full name is Equinox Delta Phillips." The crystal cleared and brightened again.

"We need no further test questions." The Queen narrowed her eyes. "You undid an enchantment of mine, a binding on a creature who betrayed my trust eons ago."

"Yes, Your Majesty." The crystal stayed bright and clear.

"You did this to stop their attack while they worked under the command of a Summoner." One of her perfectly shaped eyebrows went up, hinting that she doubted that statement.

"That's true, Your Majesty." My guilt and the reason for it was crystal-clear to everyone. I heard more shutter snaps, and flashes glittered like the wings of carpenter ants all over the audience.

"You let the Sprite, a convicted criminal amongst my people, leave without attempting to apprehend them or informing the Seelie court." She tilted her head slightly, and I noticed the tresses beside her face quivering although there was no breeze. Great Goblin's Garters, but she was angry. That was the exact moment my give-a-damn busted.

"Yes, Your Highness." I felt a flush of heat rise in my cheeks. I wasn't embarrassed. Instead, my anger matched hers.

"You will state your reasons for that decision." Her glare threatened to pin me to the spot, unable to speak. I couldn't just tell everyone here what I thought, but if I lied, the crystal would show it—and any falsehood would give the Queen a reason to slap me with the worst possible sentence.

"Fine, Your Highness. Your enchantment was torture. Looking at that Spite was like standing next to a polluted river. I'm a Kelpie. We don't abide that kind of thing. Water runs free, and I can't bear to see anyone or anything bound that way. So I broke the bonds, exactly like my ancestors used to break down dams. And then I saw how mangled the Sprite was. Their wings are just rags now. They'll never fly again. I couldn't bear to cause them any more anguish, even indirectly. Your Majesty."

The clear crystal gleamed so brightly I couldn't look at it. Neither could the Queen, judging by her lowered eyelids though I doubted the crowd could tell from a distance. But Ichiro-san noticed, too. I watched one side of his mouth tilt the tiniest bit and the corner of his eyes crinkle. No one spoke until the light dimmed back down to normal.

"Very well." The Queen turned sideways as though about to leave. Then she looked over her shoulder. "One more." I could tell from the flare of her nostrils and the set of her jaw that this last bit was the most important to her.

"Yes, Your Highness."

"A Selkie pelt went missing a few years ago. You know something of its whereabouts."

"No, Your Majesty." The crystal grayed out on the first syllable. My mouth dropped open. At least it wasn't black. A hush fell over the entire crowd. I began to understand. I did know something, but I'd thought it was all speculation until that moment.

"You will tell me all you have heard and deduced of the missing Selkie pelt."

"It got lost in a car accident on a bridge, Your Majesty. That was in the papers back then, which anyone can check. It belonged to a drunkard, the man who caused the accident. That pelt has nothing to do with me." The crystal stayed bright and clear this time.

"And where is it now?" The armed attendants fingered their necklaces and rubbed their bracelets. If I lied now, a fight might break out.

"I…hold on." I raised my chained hands to rub my forehead. I'd been about to say I didn't know, but maybe our guesses in the lounge had been correct. "I think someone has it. Someone could have picked it up that night. There's been a Selkie around lately, too." I had to think harder, figure it out. I wasn't Lynn Frampton or Blaine Harcourt, but neither of them had been at Swan Point that night. I'd have to rely on my own wits instead of borrowing theirs.

"You will tell me who has it." The Queen turned to face me again.

A flight of gasps escaped the crowd as two attendants guarding the nearest aisle moved aside for no one. It was like they'd been unaware they'd done it until other people noticed. Now that was a mystery I could solve because I'd seen it before. Umbral magic. More than one someone had just walked past the guards under its cloaking effects. Was this some attempt to break me out? I wouldn't go.

A murky shimmer appeared like a smudge in mid-air. It melted away until I could see Maddie May standing next to a smiling Kimiko and a man with beige skin, hazel eyes, tawny sun-bleached hair, and more lines than I ever thought I'd see on his face. The salty tang of the ocean met my nose so strongly I sneezed. Here was my answer.

"Ren Ichiro, Your Majesty. He's got the Selkie pelt. We thought he'd died in the accident, but he must have used the pelt to save his own life." Ren and Kimiko rushed to their dad's side for a big group hug.

"Equinox Delta Phillips, you are guilty as charged of breaking my enchantment and of no other crime. Your solicitor will negotiate your sentence with me before his family reunion progresses further." The Queen beckoned, and Ichiro-san followed her. The Brownie accompanied me as I hurried to talk to Maddie.

"Where's Josh?"

"I don't know." She glanced around and saw the two empty seats. "He should be here. I just came from repaying that favor to Gee Nome. I had to hide Ren and bring him here because

Gnomes are at risk around this many Seelies. But I haven't seen Josh or Blaine since last night."

I shivered, peering at the empty seats. Over where the cars had parked, the Harcourt limousine had just pulled up. I squinted since the sun was in my eyes. A woman strode down the hill, holding a burlap sack in one hand and an oilcloth pouch in the other. Hertha Harcourt. She went straight to Lynn, whispering something in her ear. Lynn went deadly pale, her eyes flicking to me. Then, she shook her head. I saw her mouth the word "No." Hertha murmured, opening the bag. Lynn went an unhealthy shade of green. She shut her eyes and shuddered. Bobby put his arm around her. Olivia put her hands on her cheeks. Beth froze like a statue, hands gripping her elbows. Maddie nudged me, then jerked her chin at the limo.

Josh had finally arrived. Blaine and Mr. Harcourt supported him between them. His feet dragged furrows in the grass. He sweated despite the brisk temperature, lips an unhealthy shade of blue. His eyes met mine, and he gave me a grim grin. My injured knees wobbled, threatening to buckle. Maddie grabbed my arm. The Brownie snapped the chain between my manacles. I glanced up to see Mrs. Harcourt handing an oilcloth pouch out to the Queen. I couldn't bring myself to care. Josh looked like death.

"Go." The Brownie's voice was low and not unkind. Maybe they weren't just a stick bug.

By that time, it wasn't far to Josh's side. Blaine and his dad put him on the ground, and I stretched out next to him. My stupid leg wounds made it impossible to squat.

"You're a mess, Dennison."

"Just getting you out of one, Phillips." His voice was raspy, and his eyes looked hollow. He shivered. "Your sentencing done?"

"Not just yet."

"I need to see that, know you're okay."

"No. You need rest."

"I can rest when you're safe." He closed his eyes. When he

opened them again, they were that amber wolf color. "And maybe I'll even haunt you for a while."

"Why are you talking like that?"

"I'm dying. Cockatrice venom. No antidote. Even the brainiac doesn't know of one." He shuddered. I reached out to smooth his hair.

"There has to be some way." I shook my head, tears cold against the hot rise of defiant anger.

"One." I looked up. Ren stood over us. "Water magic can purify his blood, but we'd need to be extremely lucky to pull that kind of spell off. And we have to work together, even with the opposing Faerie energy."

"I can't help." The words came out as a growl. "Queen's got my pelt."

"No, she doesn't." Blaine stood there, holding a familiar oilcloth pouch. "She's got *a* pelt. This one's yours. The one my mom's handing over, not so much." Blaine shrugged. "Put it on and save your man, Equinox." He smirked.

"What about the Luck?" I took the pelt out of the pouch and pressed it to my stomach.

"Covered." Kimiko held something small and gleaming in her hand. "Lifted it off Dad at just the right time. Lucky, huh?" She held the lapel pin. Of course, a Tanuki lawyer would wear a Luck charm at trial. Its golden glow confirmed my earlier suspicions.

"It better be." I called to the water nearby and under the ground as I had at the fight the night before. Ren had already put one hand on Josh's right wrist and the other on his ankle. I mirrored him. I knew from my coursework that the Seelie and Unseelie energies in our Water magic would act like opposing magnets. If we did this right, we'd flush the cockatrice's venom right out of Josh's system.

We focused, each murmuring words under our breath, Ren's in Japanese and mine in a surprising mix of Gaelic and some other tongue I didn't recognize. One of my ancestors had done this before, but he was so far back in line I'd never heard him until now. I shut my eyes, trying to see his face in my mind's eye to get a better grasp of his knowledge. He'd been an ocher-skinned man with gleaming straight black hair and high cheekbones. His eyes twinkled, so dark a brown they were nearly black, like chips of obsidian in terra cotta clay. Now I understood why Taki Waban had given me the church-keys. Somewhere way back, we were related.

Josh's sweating went into overdrive, now tinged with green. The poison and water we flushed it with had to go somewhere. The longer we worked, the more color came back into his cheeks, although his eyes were still hollow, and his lips stayed blue. My whole body drooped, limbs heavy. My pelt's magic had also gone toward healing my legs, enough to make me worry I'd run out of steam before Josh was out of the woods. I glanced at Ren, looking for some sign. He shook his head and looked at Kimiko.

She sat at Josh's feet, holding the pin in her cupped hands. She seemed to be waiting for something. When Josh started seizing, she acted. A gilt glimmer rose from her hands, dissipating as it went. She blew gently on the shimmering air in front of her, tilting her fingertips to point at Josh's feet. Golden motes wafted down over him, Ren, and me. A renewed surge of magic rushed over me like a big roller down at Scarborough Beach. Josh threw his head back, then broke Ren's grip. He turned on his side, brackish water gushing from his nose and mouth.

When he pushed up from the ground, he sighed. There was no more blue around his lips, and his skin was back to its normal shade. He still had those dark circles under his eyes, but I'd take it. He flung his arms around me. I hugged him back so tightly, Grandpa got on my case about not breaking his ribs.

"Why don't *you* bring girls like this home, Blaine?" I glanced up at Mrs. Harcourt. She wasn't looking at me. Josh pulled me in for a kiss before I could figure out who she was talking about.

"They turn me down." Blaine snorted. "They're right, too, Mother."

When I could look around again, the Queen and her attendants were gone, along with the truth crystal. So were the Ichiros. The Harcourts brought everyone back to campus. They dropped me, Beth, and Josh back at the Dennisons'. I could have slept for days, but only got until the next morning.

CHAPTER NINETEEN

Josh

"I can't believe you're stuck in my old wheelchair." Beth set the glass with vodka and orange juice in it on the table in front of me. I glanced up and around, glad I'd been able to get down to the basement in this contraption. I don't think I could have handled another minute of being coddled by my parents upstairs.

"Yeah, but only for a couple more days." I sipped the tart beverage, glad I wasn't on any painkillers. Vodka tasted so much better than horse pills. "Leaping Luna! I missed my exam."

"I think the Headmistress will insist they let you make it up." Bobby sat across from me, steadily putting away bagels with cream cheese and lox.

"Yeah, you were on the Psychic News Network and everything." Lynn made more bagels topped with cream cheese and lox, keeping one for herself and passing the rest to Bobby.

"That was a Hail Mary pass, Hertha Harcourt coming out of left field like that with another Kelpie pelt." Fred opted for donuts instead of the bagels, inhaling a half-dozen of them. "You'd have died if she'd taken Nox's."

"Equinox, you mean." Blaine leaned back in his chair, smoke rising steadily from his nose. "I can't let anyone forget that's her real name."

"Jeez, you're worse than my brother." Beth elbowed him, then pointed at the Dark and Stormy in front of him. "You're not drinking that?" She reached for the glass.

"Not right now." Blaine shooed her away. "Just watching the fizz go out of it."

"You're an oddball, you know that, right?" Beth rolled her eyes and headed over to the bar to make her own drink.

"So, I think it's time to let Fred in on all of this." I drummed my fingers on the table. "Tell it, Trogdor."

"I'll let someone else do it for a change if it's all the same to you, Grand High Poobah." Blaine's eyes tracked his glass. Up, down. Up, down. I'd leave him to it for now, considering he'd saved Nox.

"Fine." I filled Fred in on the Extramagus situation, Lynn and Bobby chiming in from time to time.

"So now that this is over and you and Nox are okay, who's next?" Fred reached for more donuts, but they were all gone.

"Don't go eating the furniture, Fred." Olivia swept in from the backyard with a handful of bags. "Looks like I made it back from Dunkin just in time. Hoo boy." She set the bags on the table in front of the Redcap. "What did I walk in on?"

"Evil bad guy out to get us." Fred only had eyes for the bags full of pastries. "I'm on board."

"And you're trying to figure out who's next?" Olivia blinked, perching on a chair at the bar. "That's easy. The Harcourts."

"Yup." Blaine still watched the bubbles rise and burst. "Smart owl is smart, but she doesn't know everything."

"So enlighten me, oh great and scaly one." Olivia turned

toward Blaine, leaning over the arm of her chair. But the dragon only shook his head in answer.

"The Extramagus never goes after just one person." I hadn't heard Tony come in. He watched Olivia intently, his eyes moving from her to the space between her and Blaine, as though measuring it. "It can't just be our Trogdor he's after."

"Cat-man said it." Blaine's eyes stayed glued to the glass. "No idea who it'd be in all this mess, though."

"I've got one." Lynn swallowed her mouthful of bagel. "Ren Ichiro. Nox couldn't have saved Josh without him."

"No way." Beth leaned against the bar, sipping rum-laced ginger ale. "I read through your notes last night. The bad guy can't touch Ren or me. I think the bridge was his doing."

"Hmm. Good point." Lynn shrugged with one shoulder, swallowing more bagel. "Gee Nome? Other than that, I've got nothing for now. You must be relieved Ren's safe, huh?"

Beth opened her mouth. Before she could speak, Nox rushed through the door and up to me, flinging her arms around my neck. I wheeled the chair back from the table, then pulled her into my lap. I might be too weak to stand or walk for more than a minute or two, but that didn't stop me from appreciating my mate. And I almost forgot about everyone else until the sound of a slap rang through the room.

"I don't want to see your face around here, Ren Ichiro." My sister stood face to face with the man she'd have married last spring, staring daggers into his eyes. His face bore a distinct red hand-print. Nox pressed a finger to the bottom of my chin, pushing my jaw back to a more dignified closed position.

"I'm sorry, Beth." Ren didn't hang his head. He just kept on looking her in the eye. "I should have—"

"Should have what? Told me you were alive? Told your dad, so he didn't spend a fortune on your funeral? Told poor Kimiko, so she didn't have dead brother damage just like me? I can't believe you put us through all that for three years, and then you waltz in here like it never happened. I can't listen to this now." She took a step toward him, and he walked backward. "Don't bother leaving." My sister stepped around the only man she'd ever loved and headed out the way Olivia had come in. The door shook in its frame after her.

Ren stood there, looking more lost at sea than I'd imagined he'd been when I thought he was dead. He blinked a few times, then took a deep breath. He sat on one of the barstools, gazing wistfully at Beth's forgotten drink.

"So, you lived on that boat that's been in the harbor all winter, huh?" Tony shuffled over to sit next to Ren, pushing the drink down the bar. "Good call, all things considered. It's what I would have done."

"Um, yeah. Lived on it for three years, actually." Ren nodded. "Been all up and down the east coast in that old thing."

"For the record, I know why you didn't say anything." I sipped my screwdriver. "Wolf neutrality. Beth would have lost you, anyway."

"Um, you have a Kelpie on your lap, though." He scratched his head. "Aren't your parents going to have an issue with that?"

"None at all," I smirked. "With a Selkie and a Kelpie as in-laws, we have balance. Beth'll come around. She just needs time."

"Dude, she slapped him." Fred blinked. "You can't be serious."

"Yeah, and she also said she can't listen. *Right now*." I shrugged. "I know my sister. So do Mom and Dad. She'll hash things out with you eventually, Ren. But I'm warning you, your apology had better be Oscar-worthy when she does."

"Okay, but what about your pack? No balance there."

"Coincidence will take care of that. We'll find a Seelie member soon enough."

"Might have to make that two." Fred grimaced. His stomach rumbled, and for a moment, his glamour dropped. His skin was grayer than only a week ago, his ears pointier. "I have to tithe by the end of the semester, and that might be pushing it."

"Yeah, and when you do, you'll be in the Under for a year and a day." All newly tithed Changelings had to serve their Monarch for that amount of time to prove their loyalty and learn to control the extra power that came with Court alignment. "I'll have time to find someone to balance you out."

"But you've got me." Nox snuck a sip of my drink, then wrinkled her nose. "Balancing out the bad Unseelie influence on your pack is a bit overdue."

"So, what do you say, Ren?" I raised an eyebrow. "You already work well with at least one of my packmates, and I heard you talking to Headmistress Thurston about resuming your studies. I know you'll be around, and we have the smartest students here if you need study buddies."

"Um, sure." Ren glanced around the room. "But I only see one genius at the table." I hadn't noticed until then that Blaine's seat was empty. The dragon shifter had left the building.

I couldn't blame him. I wasn't sure we'd see much of him until after spring break. Even though I hadn't hidden in my house when I thought the Extramagus was after me, Blaine Harcourt probably would.

Once everyone was full of donuts, bagels, and beverages, they trailed out one by one. Nox put bottles away while I wheeled around the room, gathering napkins and paper plates to put in the trash bin. Tony stood in a corner, so still and quiet I hadn't noticed him at first.

"Go on, cat man. Shoo." I waved toward the door. "Isn't someone opening a can of tuna somewhere?"

"Nice joke. I've never heard that one before." He shook his head. "Look, I might as well say this in front of Nox, too."

"Say what in front of me?" She clinked the rum bottle back on the shelf and strode over.

"Just dropping some information to keep a promise." He shrugged. "I'm the one who woke you up the night of the new moon, Josh."

"Wait, what?" I couldn't believe my ears. I'd had suspicions about who my benefactor had been, but couldn't imagine Tony Gitano doing anything to risk his neck for anyone else. "How?"

"Church-key." He nodded at Nox. "You're not the only one who's gotten a present or few from Taki Waban."

"But why?" I shook my head, trying to reconcile the idea of Tony as a hero while dismissing my suspicion that the dragon librarian had warned me.

"You still don't understand." He sighed. "Look, your uncle Jake has some scary connections. It's why your mom didn't give him the pack when she married your dad. I mean, haven't you ever thought it was weird she kept on running it even through having three kids?"

"I just thought she was a liberated woman?" I narrowed my eyes, uncomfortable with the fact that a cat shifter seemed to know more about my extended family than I did.

"I'm sure she is. But there's more to it than that. More than even I'm completely certain of."

"And why should I believe you?"

"You don't have to if you don't want to." He shrugged. "I'm just putting it out there. Your family's not so great at keeping secrets because your parents are so upstanding. It's rare around here."

I growled. Nox put her hands on my shoulders.

"Look, I mean no disrespect, but an Extramagus with a superiority complex isn't the only player in this game we keep getting caught up in. When the big fish are after chum, the bottom feeders follow them. I think maybe you should be informed about stuff Lynn and Blaine can't find out in the library."

"Not now." I shook my head, suddenly completely exhausted. Near-death-by-poisoning could do that to a person. "Some other time."

"Okay, boss." Tony stepped sideways, closing the distance between himself and the door. "Just don't wait too long. Not knowing what I have to say almost took you out of the game before it started this time. And I don't have any more church-keys to get you out if something like that happens again."

"I've got one." Nox's lips made a thin, straight line. "Tell me. But later. You get some rest, Josh. I have an exam to take."

"Sure, horsefeathers." I rubbed my eyes, trying to stay awake long enough to hear what Tony might say. When I took my hands away, he was already gone.

Nox helped me to the couch and got me comfortable. Then she left for her exam. Finally in the quiet, I slept.

CHAPTER TWENTY

Nox

I filled in the last bubble on the scantron sheet, then got up and left as quietly as I could. I'd never ace Watkins' test, but at least I'd pass it. There would be time to make up points after Spring Break. When I got outside, I looked up at the sky, amazed at how blue it was. I headed back toward Josh's house. On the way, I heard something so beautiful it stole my breath. I closed my eyes, feet moving along the sidewalk toward the sound of a violin sweeter than honey and more entangling than spider shifter silk. I'd heard it before, felt the same compulsion the night I ran into Josh. This time, he wasn't here to distract me from following it.

I opened my eyes, trying to stop. I couldn't. Despite the early spring sun and balmy temperature, I had a bad feeling, like the night Dad didn't come home. Instead of Hope Street, I'd turned down Camp toward Rochambeau. I made it all the way to the park where I'd gotten into all this mess, feeling like I was falling toward something. And I had an idea this might be how a fly felt on its way to the bottom of a pitcher plant.

I crossed Rochambeau, turning up the drive of a yellow triple-decker house I'd been to before. At the door, I rang the bell with the name Kazynski next to it and waited. The music stopped, but before I could bolt the door opened. A frail and wizened man, bald except for a semi-circle of fuzz behind his ears greeted me.

"Miss Phillips, please. I must speak with you." His voice was heavily accented, either Russian or Polish.

"Haven't you ever heard of email?" I leaned in the doorway. "I don't appreciate being compelled. So talk already."

"This was the only safe way. You must bring this to your Alpha." He held out an old wooden box, carved all over with flowers. When I touched it, it tingled with enchantment I couldn't identify. I suspected the box itself wasn't enchanted, but the item inside absolutely was. Strong, too.

"What's it for?"

"Safekeeping. It'll open when the time comes, and he'll know what to do with it then." Old Mr. Kazynski reached out to close the door. His forearm was marked with a line of numbers. He couldn't be old enough to have been in a Concentration Camp, could he? I sniffed, realizing he was something more than just plain human.

Stopping to think had cost me the chance to ask anything else. I'd have rung again, but the old fellow seemed so frightened. Still, I hesitated. After the last few weeks, I'd gotten tired of enigmas and danger. As I lifted my finger to press the button next to his name, Mr. Kazynski started playing again. This time, the music moved me away, like the songs they play when a nightclub's about to close. I tucked the box inside my jacket and turned right onto the sidewalk.

I headed up Rochambeau toward Hope Street, crossing and making the turns down side-streets to take me to Josh's house. Men were working, replacing the old iron gates with steel replicas. I hurried up the driveway, then around the side of the house to the basement entrance.

Josh sat up on the sofa, looking around until he saw me. Then, he smiled. I went over, sitting next to him. He leaned in, kissing me. I almost forgot about the box until he pulled me closer and bumped it.

"What's that?"

I told him. He sat for a few moments, running his fingers over the wooden carvings. He set it on the coffee table. Josh put his arms around me, moving in for another kiss. When we came up for air, I leaned against his chest.

"Doesn't it drive you nuts, not knowing what's in there?" I held him close, but gently. I felt lucky to be able to hold him at all, considering he was the first wolf shifter I'd heard of to survive a cockatrice scratch.

"Nope." He ran one hand through my hair while the other caressed my back. "I'll see when it's time. For now, I've got everything I need right here."

I tilted my head to look up at him, understanding completely. Whatever came at us, we'd handle it together.

THE ACADEMY ISN'T

A Providence Paranormal College Short Story

THE ACADEMY ISN'T

"I'm not going back there, and you can't make me."

"You'll do as I say," Yoshi Ichiro crossed his arms, forcing his face into the sterner lines his daughter needed to see on it. "But it is up to you to tell me your side of things before I make my final decision regarding your attendance at The Academy."

"I hate it there." Kimi always led with her emotion, something she'd have to either outgrow or learn to use if she wanted to be a long-lived Tanuki instead of the kind that ran out of Luck in the prime of life.

"You know better than to let hatred rule your mind." Yoshi shook his head, letting a mask of disappointment hide his fear for her. "Give me better reasoning than that or back you go."

"They teach nothing there that I don't already know." Kim twirled a lock of her hair. "I can't stand how strict it is, but the worst part is that it's so..." She tugged the hair, grimacing. "*Remedial*."

"So you are bored."

"The Academy isn't for someone like me."

"I'd say it's more that someone like you isn't for The Academy." Ren leaned in the doorway. Just seeing him there hurt Yoshi's heart. He'd changed so drastically without growing much.

His son had taken after his late wife, Sora, a Telepathic Psychic. He'd been entirely mundane, too, a common occurrence in Tanuki families, but he'd come back with a Selkie pelt after going missing for three years. The Ichiro family dynamic had changed after Sora's death, and here it was, turning in an entirely different direction.

"Please, Ren," Yoshi indicated the empty space on the sofa. "Sit down and add to the discussion."

"Okay." After taking a seat, Ren leaned forward. He appeared more interested in this conversation than Kimi herself.

"I'm just dying to hear what the absentee brother thinks of the school he hasn't even seen." Kimiko rolled her eyes.

If her stinging remark bothered Ren, he didn't show it. "Well, it sounds like a fine institution. But from the way you talk about it, sending you there is like trying to make a bird live inside an aquarium."

"It's the only school that would have her, with the grades she made in her last two years of High School." Yoshi couldn't measure his tone. Something panged in his chest, on the left. Hiding that pain took more effort than he'd expected.

"See? Even Ren thinks it's the same difference, Daddy." Though she'd usually glance off to the side to accompany such a dismissive remark, Yoshi's daughter watched him like their cat watched the robins nesting in the yew bush beside the parlor window.

"It's not." Yoshi kept his mouth still and flat but couldn't stop the hidden smile from crinkling the corners of his eyes. Despite his pain, having both of his children back with him was a blessing he hadn't dreamed of. "Once you figure out why those are not precisely the same, you will understand why I sent you there to begin with."

"Why can't you just tell me?" This time, Kimi did look away.

"You gave me the impression you're bored at The Academy because all of its answers are too easy for you to get."

Kimiko opened and shut her mouth, saying nothing. His daughter was a brilliant trickster, exactly as he'd been at her age. And tradition demanded that Yoshi be as inscrutable and maddening as his own parents had been with him ages ago. Without the challenge of mystery, an intellect like hers would only stagnate. Too much depended on her putting all the right pieces together soon, including his own life. though neither of his children knew that as yet.

And he couldn't interfere without risking coincidence turning Luck in favor of the wrong people. He was stuck under the same restrictions as the other experienced adults connected to the Extramagus. Because they'd once been allies, coincidence dictated that none of them could directly cross the rising power again. If any of the older generation dared such a thing, they'd risk convergence altering all the Precognitive work done decades ago.

"Daddy, I want to learn more than what the Academy has to teach me. Isn't that enough of a reason not to send me back there?"

"So tell me then, what do you want to learn?" Yoshi's fresh bout of chest pain only made him sit up straighter, defying it.

"I'm not sure."

"Once you've figured that out, come and talk to me. I will allow you to take the rest of this semester off, but if you have not decided by the end of May, we'll have trouble planning another course of education for you."

"Okay, Daddy."

A buzzer went off, its low atonal hum stretching longer than it should have by Yoshi's estimation. The throbbing stab in his chest reached a tipping point, then ran like a stream from a mountain spring. A chill came to his bones, one he'd never quite felt before.

"That's the fish." Ren turned his head, his body following until he was halfway across the parlor to the kitchen.

The cat leapt into Yoshi's lap and from there to the arm of his chair. She clung, hissing to the velvet upholstery, raising all the hair on her back, her tail an exclamation of something gone horribly wrong. But Yoshi stood anyway.

Just one more meal, one more hour with my children. He pleaded with fate itself, wanting more than it had ever offered him before. But it wasn't meant to be.

"Daddy!" Kimi caught him, her enhanced shifter strength allowing her to sweep him up in her arms as he'd done with her as a little girl. Ren's hand flew with Extrahuman speed to the phone on the wall, pressing three numbers.

"I need the EME!" Ren raised his voice into the phone, as though the volume would bring the Emergency Medical Extrahumans faster.

"He's already here." Yoshi raised one arm, pointing at the door. It trembled more than he'd expected it to.

Ren dropped the phone and pulled open the front door to find Taki Waban there. He stepped inside, carrying his old black bag. Aside from the gray at his temples, the ancient dragon appeared almost the same as Yoshi remembered him best, from their days on the Western Frontier. Taki removed his shoes and set them aside.

"Daddy, that's a dragon, not a doctor." Kimi held him closer.

"All the same, he can help."

"No, he can't." Her voice came low and soft, a murmur even her Selkie brother and the oldest dragon in the Americas might have trouble hearing. "It's your Luck running out."

Yoshi had figured he couldn't hide that from her. As Tanuki, the two of them alone could see the running and turning of Luck energies, a type of magic even dragons couldn't properly track.

"He can." Yoshi gripped his left arm, unable to stop a grimace. "Set me down and let him do what he can, Kimi."

She brought him down the hall and to his bedroom. Ren turned down the covers, then put them back up, covering Yoshi from the waist down. They both made way for Taki Waban, who perched on the edge of the bed. After setting his bag down, he opened it and produced a magipsychically-enhanced stethoscope from inside.

"Your father needs a Luck charm." Mr. Waban turned grave eyes on Ren instead of Kim as Yoshi expected. The old dragon was a master of deflection.

"On it." Ren rummaged through the top drawer of Yoshi's dresser but came up empty-handed.

"Ren." Kim stared at her hands.

"Okay, maybe in the desk." Ren crossed the room in the blink of an eye, searched again without results.

"Ren."

"At the office then."

"Ren."

"Come on, Kimi." He tugged her wrist.

"No, Ren." Her shoulders shook. "They're all gone."

Yoshi let his eyes wander from his daughter's face to his son's. This would be harder on his Ren than Kimi. He'd been hiding alone so long, missing them, while she'd been shut away fuming with anger.

"Wait." He dropped her arm. "Gone? Because of your--"

"Yeah." When she turned her head up, Kimiko's eyes glowed with brash conviction and the gold light of Luck. "But don't worry. I got this."

Fury suited both his children better than solitude, something he'd never realized until the cancer took Sora. His son would go on missing him, shutting himself away with regret at missed years. Kimi would be the one to fight for him now. But he'd known that since the day she was born.

The Precognitive who'd consulted with Providence's Extrahuman elite hadn't been wrong yet. Lady Luck help them all if she proved fallible this time.

DRAGON MY HEART AROUND

The series continues with Dragon My Heart Around coming May 13, 2021.

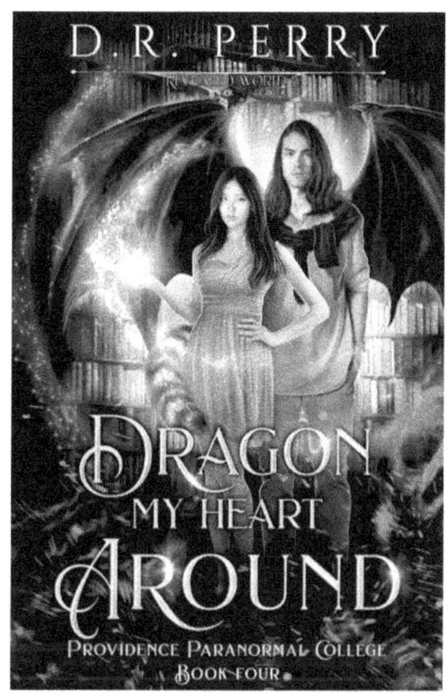

CONNECT WITH THE AUTHOR

Find D.R. Perry Online

Website: https://drperryauthor.com/

Author Central: http://www.amazon.com/-/e/B00O6851HO

Facebook: https://www.facebook.com/drpperry/

Mailing List: https://app.mailerlite.com/webforms/landing/p9i8u6

Twitter: https://twitter.com/DRPerry22

OTHER LMBPN PUBLISHING BOOKS

To be notified of new releases and special promotions from LMBPN publishing, please join our email list:

http://lmbpn.com/email/

For a complete list of books published by LMBPN please visit the following pages:

https://lmbpn.com/books-by-lmbpn-publishing/

www.ingramcontent.com/pod-product-compliance
Lightning Source LLC
LaVergne TN
LVHW010617100826
845148LV00014B/3003

* 9 7 8 1 6 4 9 7 1 7 0 0 9 *